# WHO THREW THAT COCONUT!

*A Book By Jerry Colonna*

With A Foreword By Bob Hope

Cover And Cartoons By Sig Vogt

Published in the USA by:
BearManor Media
PO Box 1129
Duncan, Oklahoma 73534-1129
*www.bearmanormedia.com*

ISBN 978-1-59393-552-8

Book Production by Brian Pearce | Red Jacket Press.

THIS IS A VERY GOOD BOOK

NBC
SIG VOGT

# FOREWORD

## by BOB HOPE

*SOME weeks ago, while I was engaged in the delicate work of injecting a little rocket fuel into my golf balls, the door of my study was flung open and Professor Colonna burst in, screaming.*

*"I did it! I did it! Just what you told me to do!"*

*I couldn't imagine what he was talking about. Did he swipe that Oscar for me? Did he splinter Crosby's niblick? Before I could ask the question, he shoved a manuscript into my hands.*

*"There it is, Hope. I wrote it. You read it."*

*I have known Jerry Colonna man and mustache for seven years, so you can understand how surprised I was when he showed me his book. I had expected hieroglyphics.*

*Even now it is hard for me to imagine what little springs clicked the tumblers in that weird brain to evolve the delightful bits of fantasy you will find in the following pages. It all started in the South Pacific where our troupe went to entertain your boys. It was all good fun and the fellows seemed to enjoy it. For a few short hours they had a chance to relax and enjoy a mental furlough from the job of taking the Hiro out of Hito.*

*After a few weeks with the troops, the military way of doing things became second nature to us. Whenever the Professor had something to say to me, I told him to put it in writing and make seven copies. I have just read what he wanted to tell me all that summer. No man can escape his fate.*

*As for the seven copies, Colonna accentuated the negative and as a result there are several hundred thousand of these reports cluttering up the book stores of the nation.*

*Not many people thought Colonna could write a book, but there are two sides to the Professor. One is the zany, silly moron, and the other is the deep-thinking, serious moron. Don't get me wrong. Colonna's really got a head on his shoulders—thanks to plastic surgery.*

*We met quite by accident. It seems we were driving in opposite directions on a one-way street.*

*Most people get off easy in an accident. They sprain an ankle or break an arm. I met Jerry Colonna.*

*He claimed he had the right of way, and I claimed I had the right of way. Then a cop came along and we both had to remove our cars from the sidewalk.*

*I told Colonna he would have to pay for the damages he had done to my car. He agreed to settle just as soon as he got a job. That's how Jerry Colonna came to work on my program. This was one of the best moves I ever made. Colonna has paid me back more than a hundred-fold. Every month we meet on that same one-way street.*

*My next best move was to ask the Professor to compile this hilarious record of the madder aspects of our South Pacific trip. I'm sure you'll enjoy browsing through the melange of cartoons and memoirs which, when taken to bed, serves as a nice introduction to a nightmare.*

*My boy, Tony, said it was the best book he ever picked up. Of course, he can't read yet. He's four.*

*My girl, Linda, was skeptical. She can read. She's five. She glanced at the first page, put Colonna's book down, and said:*

*"Whatsa matter? Is he crazy or something?"*

Bob Hope

# DEDICATION

*I HAVE eaten ice cream in Puvuvu, bummed a cigaret from a six-foot Polynesian in Majuro, and siphoned gas in Espiritu Santo Island in the New Hebrides. Today Main Street runs right through the middle of the South Sea Isles.*

*A Maori chieftain summed it up for me:*

*"After war, maybe Marines go. Maybe ships go. Maybe airplanes go. But chewing gum here to stay."*

*The Pacific Islands will never forget the American soldier. And his good humor and playfulness will be remembered as long as his courage and efficiency. To the baseball games on Guadalcanal, the moving pictures in the jungle, the cartoons on the bombers, and the wise cracks under fire—this book is dedicated.*

# INTRODUCTION

*WHEN Bob Hope appointed me official chronicler of our Pacific tour, I was thrilled. My eyes sparkled, my lips grinned, my mustache curled, and my ears wiggled in unison. What a production!*

*We had just returned from the islands. Bob was making a picture, doing his weekly thirty minutes of banter over the air, giving camp shows all over the country, writing a daily newspaper column, and preparing a new book. He slept an hour every other week, and only ate for sentimental reasons.*

*"You write about Kauai, Noumea, Pitylu, and Nadzab," he told me. "I can't even take time out to pronounce them."*

*So, typewriter in hand, I sat down to write a book. For three hours I sat there. "Ah!" I muttered to myself. "Now we're getting nowhere."*

*I remained glued to my chair staring at the typewriter. All I could think of was the peculiar word, QWERTYUIOP. Where did I get this inspiration? Simply by reading across the second line of keys.*

*Suddenly a sharp sensation shot through my brain. An idea? No! My little son, Robert John, had crept into my study and accidentally let his toy B29 glide into my right ear.*

*"What are you doing, daddy?" said Robert John.*

*"What else? Writing a book."*

*"Egad, dad! That's sad!"*

*"Why, lad?"*

*"Are you mad?"*

*I thought it time to terminate this irreverent conversation. Besides, I could think of no rhyme for "mad."*

*Putting Robert John in his place—in the backyard—I recommenced my literary labors. I reviewed in my mind our trip to the South Pacific. While my brain was thus engaged, my fingers, for lack of anything else to do, started typing out my memoirs.*

*The result is recorded in these pages. Please let me know how my fingers made out.*

Jerry Colonna

# U. S. O. UNIT—No. 130

FRANCES LANGFORD, singer—beaut!

PATTY THOMAS, dancer—cute!

JERRY COLONNA, professor—brute!

TONY ROMANO, guitarist—keen!

BARNEY DEAN, with pate so clean!

BOB HOPE, Oh, you know what I mean!

Hello Hope

THE telephone rang.

It was a warm summer day and I was out in my garden trimming the shrubbery. They wouldn't let me shave in the house.

The telephone rang again.

Persistent little beast, that telephone. It always catches me indisposed. Ah! but this time I fooled it. It caught me in the garden.

I rushed into the house, picked up the receiver, and in my best pear-shaped tones opened the conversation:

"Hello?"

"Hello, Colonna?"

That voice! The voice that took an ordinary day in the week and made it Tuesday Night. I repeated, "Hello!"

He said, "Hello, Colonna."

That's what I like about Hope, always ad libbing.

To verify my suspicions I said, "Is this Bob Hope, the famous comedian, picture star, and author of the best seller, 'I Never Left Home'?"

"I didn't hear you, Colonna. Please repeat that."

I told him if I did, it would cost him another ten.

He said never mind, and changed the subject. He has always found that easier than changing a twenty.

"Colonna," he said, "we're leaving the country."

"Egad, again? I didn't think our last show was that bad."

"No, Colonna, a hundred thousand service men have signed a petition asking us to entertain the troops in the South Pacific."

I asked him where the names came from and he said from all over the United States.

"Ah, Hope," I said, "isn't it great to feel that you're wanted? Who else is going to make the trip?"

"We're going to have a great troupe, Colonna—Frances Langford, Patty Thomas, Tony Romano, and Barney Dean, and me."

"Me! Who's me?"

"Colonna!" Hope said sharply. "Get yourself together. I want you to report to the Wm. E. Branch Clinic—Vine and Yucca, tomorrow morning to be inoculated against small pox, yellow fever, typhoid, and cholera."

"Who knows, Hope, maybe they can clear up my dandruff!"

Hope snorted, "You're ridiculous!"

"No, I'm Colonna," I snapped back, "and I've got my driver's license to prove it."

Hope is easily upset. "Oh, Colonna, you wear me to a frazzle!"

The thought of wearing him to a frazzle intrigued me, but the day was too hot. I would have had to leave him in the cloak room.

I explained the situation to him and waited patiently for his reply. When I had heard nothing by sun-down, I decided that he had hung up on me. You see, I never jump at conclusions. Unless they jump at me first!

## "HI, PODERMIC"
## or
## MY INTRODUCTION TO A NEEDLE

THE next morning arrived sooner than I had expected. It caught me asleep. I glanced at my alarm clock. It had a mustache just like mine. Egad, nine-fifteen! I was already late for my appointment to get my overseas shots. I rushed around like mad. Of course Mad got very angry—he said I was always copying him.

I dressed hurriedly and dashed out of the

house where I had to fight my way through a crowd of autograph hunters. This always upsets me. I wish Van Johnson didn't live next door. He doesn't really live next door. He lives in Beverly Hills, which is five miles away. The line goes right by my house!

Climbing into my car, I seated myself behind the wheel, put my hand out and signaled a passing cab. My car hasn't run for months.

"Where to, buddy?"

"I've got to get to the Wm. E. Branch Clinic, at once," I said.

The cab driver looked concerned. "What's the matter with you?"

"Nothing," I replied indignantly. "I've just got to get to the Clinic. I'm Professor

Colonna, of the Bob Hope Show."

He seemed amazed. "Have they got a cure for that?"

The cab driver warned me that the fare was a dollar to the Clinic. I assured him that I had a dollar-fifteen in my pocket. So he let me out a mile past the hospital. It's a good thing I didn't have two dollars on me or I would have wound up in Laguna.

When I arrived at the Clinic, I found the rest of the gang waiting to be called for their shots. Frances was tapping her foot, Patty Thomas was biting her fingernails, and Barney and Tony were nervously pacing up and down. Hope alone was calm. He lay there smiling up at me from his oxygen tent.

They all rushed at me as I entered. They were really glad to see me. I had been elected to go first.

I saw that it was up to me to calm them down. I said, "You're all acting like children. Think for a moment: What harm can a few hypodermic needles do to you?" That was all that was needed. The next thing I remember they were reviving me.

Needless to say, it was an embarrassing situation, but I passed it off with a quip: "That will give you a *faint* idea of what I mean."

A doctor stuck his head out of the door and said he was ready to start. We fellows got together and decided that the gentlemanly thing to do was let the ladies go first.

Frances went in with Patty Thomas. Patty was the dancer for Hope's U.S.O. unit. You know how Frances has a figure that speaks for itself? Well, Patty has the same thing only hers stutters in the right places.

A few minutes later the girls came out rubbing their arms and the doctor came out rubbing his jaw.

Tony Romano and Barney Dean went in next. Tony plays the guitar and accompanies Frances when she sings. Barney is a writer at Paramount. He's a very small fellow. In fact, he looks like he made a curtsey and never came out of it.

It was now Hope's turn. With a casual air he tried to hide under the sofa, but I wouldn't make room for him.

I soon discovered I was braver than Hope. It took four men to carry him in, and it took only two to handle me.

They brought me into a little room and set me down in front of the doctor. The doctor studied me for a few minutes and finally shook his head.

I exclaimed, "Unbelievable, isn't it!"

The doctor picked up my arm and took my pulse. You can't trust these doctors. They'll take anything. I told him so.

He raised his eyebrows. Have you ever tried raising eyebrows? It's more fun than raising chickens.

The doctor brought out a needle about three feet long.

"What are you going to do?" I screamed. "Spear fish?"

"Yes, *muscles,*" he said and laughed heartily.

I told him he ought to be on the radio, and I wished he was there right now.

He said, "Now, this won't hurt a bit." And he was right. He didn't feel a thing.

The last thing I recall saying was, "What's the purpose of all this? I don't get the point."

He gave it to me.

Hope rushed in. "Professor, are you ready to fly to San Francisco?"

"San Francisco!" I said. "With the fuel the Doc put in me, I'm ready to fly to Nome, Alaska.

**SAN FRANCISCO**
**or**
**WHAT MORE CAN I SAY?**
**IT'S ALL BEEN COVERED IN THE PICTURE BY THE SAME NAME**

WE were at Hamilton Field, San Francisco ready to take off for Honolulu at two-thirty A.M., Goosepimple Watch Time.

I exclaimed, "All right, gang, let's go!"

But Hope caught me just as I was jumping into a cab to take me home.

Two-thirty in the morning! What a time for a man to be going any place. Usually at two-thirty I'm fast asleep in the arms of Herb-eous. Morph is on his vacation and Herb's taking his place.

There was a C-54 waiting for us. For those of you who don't know what a C-54 looks like, please turn the page. You will see a picture of a guy who doesn't know what a C-54 looks like either.

We went into the office of Major George K. Spearman to clear our papers. The Major had me fill out the answers to a lot of questions: Name? Age? Weight? Place of Birth? and so forth. It reminded me of my high school exams. I flunked every question.

I feel that I should mention here that Major Spearman was a very considerate chap. He told us there was nothing to worry about in our flight over the Pacific.

"There'll be a few little incidentals like bailing out of the plane, swimming a couple

DUNCE
2+2=8
3
2
4
11
TEACHER
wadaya know—
no brains
REPORT CARD
Nov. 7, 1864
Dear Mrs. Colonna:—
I am at wits end—
your son Jerry needs special

of hundred miles to shore, fighting off sharks, but really nothing serious to worry about."

I knew he was trying to scare us, but I didn't blink an eye. I was too scared.

The Major said he wished he were one of us so he could go on this mission filled with adventure and danger. I suggested that Hope go speak to his Colonel and fix it up so that he could go with us. The Major suggested that I shut up.

There were still two hours to the take-off, so we just sat around waiting for things to break—like an adolescent attending his first burlesque show. I don't know if everyone was nervous or not, but I was really beside myself. Were you ever beside yourself? It's a pretty difficult trick unless you're double-jointed.

To kill time we walked over and watched them prepare the plane for flight. The men were working on the ship as though it were a matter of life and death. It was—ours.

As a gag the crew asked me to get behind the controls and see if everything met with my approval. I've always wanted to be a pilot. Colonna the aviator. It made me air-sick to think of it! I studied the instrument panel. Now I know why they call this ship a C-54. Wherever you look you see 54 different dials. I checked the RPM. Okeh! I checked the ALT. Okeh! I checked the OPA. No gas! The time had come. I yelled, "Contact!" but Contact wasn't around so Davis came in his place. He turned over the motor, and then turned it over again. It looked the same on both sides, so he put it back in the plane.

At last Hope came over and said, "This is it. We take off!"

Being a good trouper I followed orders and was down to my shorts before the girls started to scream. In the excitement, however, this minor misunderstanding was overlooked and everyone boarded the plane.

Captain Van Antwerp, the pilot, tapped me on the shoulder and explained that we weren't allowed to take any animals on the trip. I spent five minutes before I convinced him that it was a mustache.

Before I knew it the plane motors had started up. Things were always happening before I knew it. Like the girl back in St. Louis—but that's a different story.

We weren't alone on the plane. Besides our own gang there was a group of fighter pilots who were shipping out to various Pacific bases. They were young, eager kids, well trained and on the ball. We had taken all the available seats. I thought, these kids are going to war. My upper lip started twitching. Egad, I thought, I'm getting sentimental. But no. They were pulling my mustache to see if it was real.

Finally we left the ground. We had to. There wasn't enough room to take it along.

The take-off was uneventful except that I sat down on my rabbit's foot. I should have trimmed its nails before leaving.

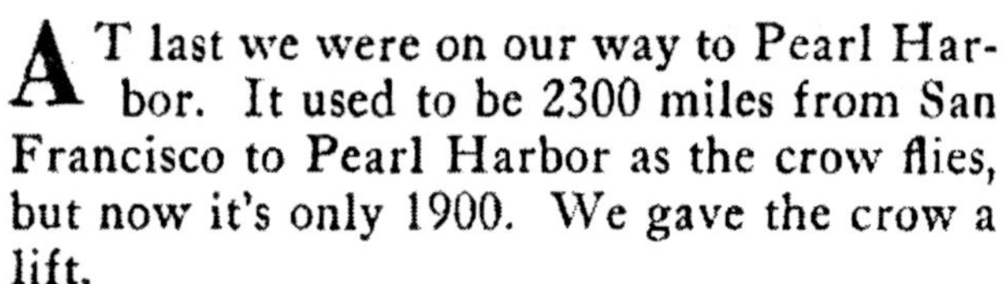

**INTO THE WILD BLUE YONDER**
**or**
**THIRTY SECONDS OVER**
**ALCATRAZ**

AT last we were on our way to Pearl Harbor. It used to be 2300 miles from San Francisco to Pearl Harbor as the crow flies, but now it's only 1900. We gave the crow a lift.

Some people are afraid of flying, but not me. I've been flying ever since the day my mother diapered me and was a little careless with the safety pin.

The first few hours of the trip were pretty rough. Then I started using my own dice. But it was a long flight and I had plenty of time on my hands. Of course, after a while they noticed it, and I had to give everybody back his wrist-watch.

I went over to where the navigator was taking some observations and looked into the sights. "Egad!" I cried, "What ghastly territory we're flying over!"

He said, "You're seeing your reflection in the glass."

I had no argument prepared, so I asked him to point out the position of the plane on the Map. Then I asked him to point out the position of the ice box on the plane. I was considering what I would make myself for lunch, but I couldn't make up my mind. Finally something struck me. It was Hope. He told me to behave myself. He made me sit down in my seat and put on my Mae West. That's a lifejacket, you know. And I must admit that in a Mae West I look like Wallace Beery.

The young fliers on the plane acted like gentlemen all during the trip. They just sat there and admired Frances and Patty from afar. Of course, Tony and Barney worked hard to hold them in their seats.

We put on a little act for the fliers during a thunder storm. However, we became a little discouraged when even the thunder wouldn't clap. It's a pitiful experience to have a bunch of guys sit and laugh at you all day, and the moment you open your mouth and say something funny—they stop.

Watching the water below us inspired me to sing. After they had heard my rendition of "How Deep Is The Ocean," the crew offered to help me find out. I spent a soul-searing half hour hanging from the bomb-bay doors.

Once we flew through a cloud bank.

I left a deposit. It gives you a strange feeling being in the center of a cloud. You can't tell whether you're upside down, right side up, or coming or going. Well, what do you know! Just like home.

The co-pilot Lieut. Ramsey shouted, "We're coming in for a landing! Fasten your life belts!" We all obeyed. Little Barney Dean nearly strangled. His belt caught him around the neck.

As we dropped through the clouds, I sighted Hawaii.

We came in for a perfect four-point landing.

Why didn't somebody tell me my legs were hanging out of the plane.

*Her grass skirt and my mustache were first cousins.*

### WE LAND
### or
### A HICK AT HICKMAN FIELD

A DELEGATION of Hawaiian notables greeted us with the traditional cry of "Aloha." Aloha can mean either hello or goodbye. In this case it meant both.

Also present to bid us welcome were Army and Navy officers as well as hula-hula dancers. We felt that the officers had come down to meet us, but we soon found out they were there to watch the hula-hula girls. It was their duty to keep their eyes on tropical movements.

We couldn't decide whether to press on to the South Pacific in three hours or three days. After watching the Hula dancers perform, we decided to press on in three weeks. Ah, those Hula dancers! Hawaii is full of them. Wherever you look you see a bunch of grass doing the Notre Dame shift. Surprising as it sounds, after five minutes I found out I was related to one of the dancers. We discovered that her grass skirt and my mustache were first cousins.

You know, there's more to these Hula dancers than meets the eye. Of course, what meets the eye isn't bad! Hula dancing is a choreographic* history of the islands. Every

*Any similarity between this word and the one in Webster's dictionary is purely coincidental.

movement of the hands spells out a historical fact. You can also pick up quite an education from the footnotes.

It began to get dark so we headed for town. Hope and I laughed and laughed at the monkeys living in the coconut trees. Then we went to the Royal Hawaiian and priced the rooms and stopped laughing at the monkeys. As we passed one tree I saw a mother monkey grab her little one and point at me. "Look," she screeched, "*Now* will you eat your bananas?" I've been trying to convince myself ever since that it was my imagination.

Realizing the monkeys wouldn't put us up for the night, (I am known throughout the world), we threw ourselves on the mercy of the manager of the Willard Inn. *He* threw us out on the street. After much dickering, we finally persuaded the manager to let us have a room overlooking the beach. He said that's not all we'd have to overlook. It was an outside room where you could see the ocean—and during the night you could feel it.

We hadn't been at the Willard long before Captain Evans came to arrange our Hawaiian schedule. He was the special service officer in that area. After a while it occurred to me that Captain Evans was Maurice Evans, the famous Shakespearian actor. After a while it occurred to him who I was—and he stuck around anyway.

I took to him immediately. Not many

people know this, but I'm a Shakespearian actor myself. I once played "King Lear." Unfortunately he ran out of the money, and Seabiscuit won. That was one of my greatest tragedies! I spent the rest of the night quoting Shakespeare from memory. Evans remarked that either Shakespeare isn't so good or my memory isn't so good.

After we had exhausted Shakespeare as well as Captain Evans, he told us that tomorrow morning we would play our first show on the nearby island of Maluhia, famous for its excellent pineapples. We decided right then and there to take our catcher's masks with us.

| U. S. O. UNIT | DATE | PLACE | AUDIENCE |
|---|---|---|---|
| *#130* | *July 12* | *Maluhia* | *10,000* |

### OUR FIRST SHOW
### or
### YOU CAN'T BE FUNNY ALL THE TIME

TODAY we rolled up our sleeves, dusted off our witty sayings, and went to work. We really had a heavy schedule. We went from camp to camp, from beach to beach, and from bad to worse.

The island of Maluhia was covered with pineapples, but this didn't impress Hope. He cracked, "What's so wonderful about a pineapple? It's just an avocado wearing a cactus for a hat."

That's the way our shows overseas went. Hope swept them off their feet. The girls swept the men off their feet. Tony Romano swept them off their feet. I got the brush.

I believe that right here I should reveal the circumstances responsible for wearing my eyebrows at half-mast. It seems that during my impetuous youth I became infatuated with a sweet young thing. Ah! she was slender, she was tall, she was different! In fact, as far as I was concerned, she was more than just different—she was indifferent! We were to be married, but she gave me the brush. I've been wearing it ever since.

One of the high spots of our show came when Frances Langford sang. The fellows loved her. To them she was "home." To me she was never home.

Tony Romano was our musical director and entire band. The sounds that boy could get out of a guitar. The rippling arpeggios when Frances sang. The cute cadenzas when Patty danced. And the crashing chords on my head when I stole his date. Egad! What an experience that was! For a week after that every time I combed my hair it sounded like "Holiday For Strings."

| U. S. O. UNIT | DATE | PLACE | AUDIENCE |
|---|---|---|---|
| *#130* | *July 13* | *Aieu Naval Hospital* | *1,000* |

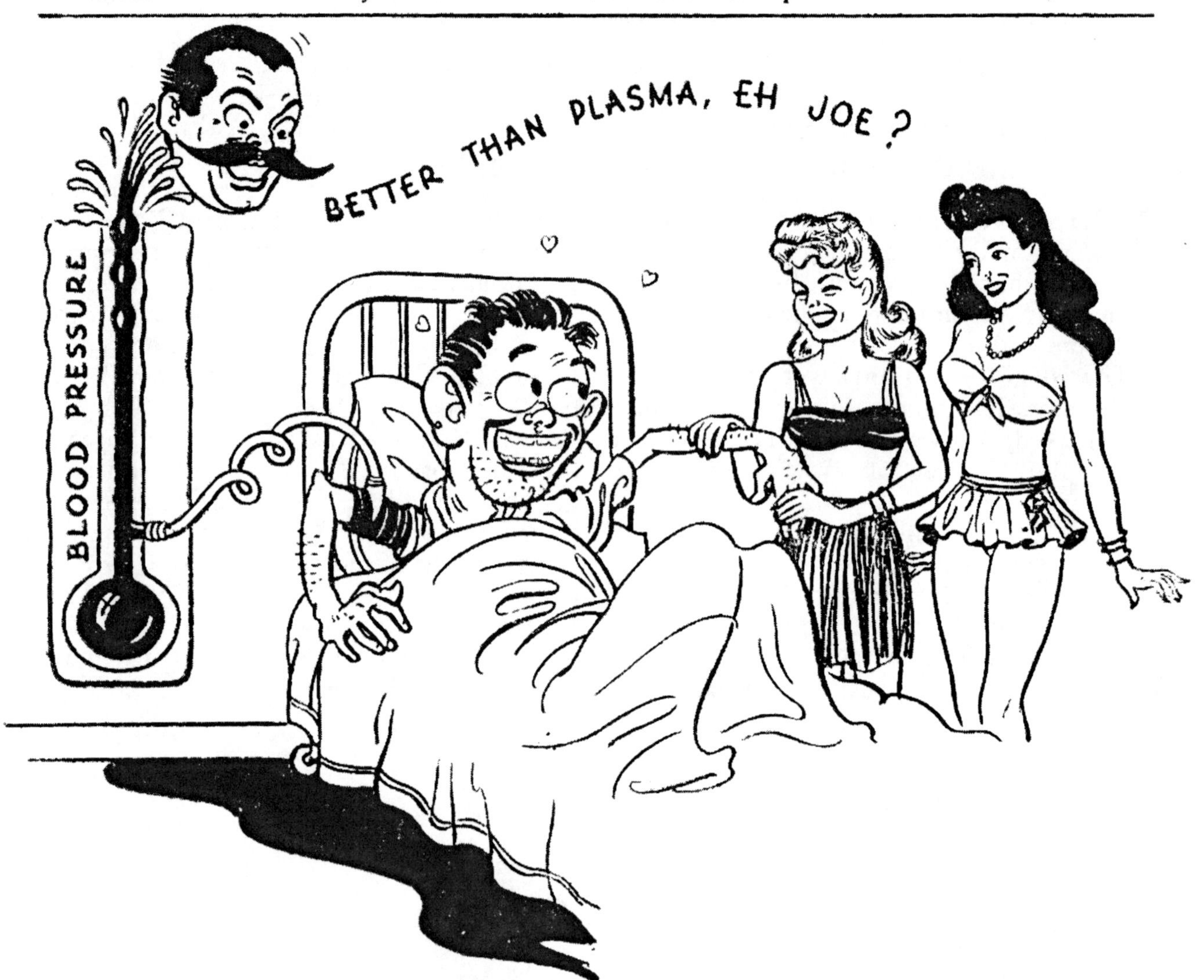


**WE ENTERTAIN AT THE HOSPITAL**
**or**
**BLOOD PRESSURE GOING UP?**

THE next morning I awoke early and went out to see the sights. I saw some beautiful sights, but they all had sailors with them. Another interesting phenomenon was my first coconut. I was rather disappointed. It was merely a bowling ball with five-o'clock shadow.

In the afternoon we visited the Aieu (pronounced "Aieu") Naval Hospital. The patients here turned out to be our best audience. They couldn't do anything but be patient.

We had arrived just as the nurses were taking the temperatures of the fellows and when Frances and Patty walked in thermometers could be heard popping all over the ward.

One thing the Japs couldn't do to these wounded veterans was damage their sense of humor. There was one colored boy in the ward whom everyone called Dallas. Needless to say it was because he came from Galveston. Dallas made a point of telling us that he was the only fellow in the hospital who never made any kicks about his treatment. "I can't," he said and pointed to his legs in a cast.

Hope and I were kidding around trading wise cracks and Hope happened to mention something about Crosby's horses. Dallas cut in with, "The only reason Crosby's horses ever come in is to eat."

Hope shook his hand. "Happy to meet anybody that's on my side."

At another bed a sailor told us he was the victim of the most unusual accident in the Navy. It seems he had laced his pants up too tight and developed combat fatigue before he could get out of them again.

All in all the fellows seemed happy that we had at last arrived in the islands. Now they knew that their loved ones at home weren't suffering.

We found out that the principal thought in each sailor's mind was still the girl back home. One bluejacket was so devoted to his girl that he wanted to give Frances something to take back to her. Frances had to refuse. She didn't have time for a thousand kisses. But she compromised by singing "I Can't Give You Anything But Love," which she dedicated to his girl.

As I strolled over to one bed, I immediately made the patient feel much better.

He looked me over a moment and then said, "I think I'll get up. If they let you walk around, I should have been out of here a month ago."

Seeing these men reminded me of my experiences in a hospital. I went there incognito. In those days they used cognitos instead of ambulances. I went up to the room, took off my clothes, donned a nightshirt, and slipped into bed. Presently the doctor arrived and looked me over sympathetically. He said I didn't have to go to all this trouble just to visit a sick friend. However, as long as I was so comfortably situated, I decided to take advantage of the facilities of the hospital. I called for my nurse, I called for my lunch, I called for my fiddlers three. I had many visitors that day. Later I learned the nurse was selling tickets to the internes just to come in and take a look at me. I was very indignant about this. I insisted that she split fifty-fifty with me.

As we left the hospital, a doctor handed us some pictures that had been taken during our act. I looked at mine and said, "This is the best picture of me that has ever been taken, but where is my mustache?"

The doctor explained that it was an X-ray.

| U. S. O. UNIT | DATE | PLACE | AUDIENCE |
|---|---|---|---|
| *#130* | *July 13* | *Nimitz Bowl* | *20,000* |
| | | *Pearl Harbor* | *20,000* |

**WE VISIT NIMITZ BOWL**
**or**
**TWO FRIGHTS AT THE FIGHTS**

AFTER we had filled our engagements at Aieu (if you think it's hard to pronounce, try it backwards), the Special Service officer, Lieut. John Margraf, told us that we had been working pretty hard, and now was our relaxation period. I sat down, he said, "Time's up!", and we were on our way again. We had an appointment to attend a boxing show at Nimitz Bowl. I would much rather have crawled into bed, but when you're with the Navy, you relax the way they tell you.

We hadn't been seated for more than a minute when word got around that Bob Hope and Colonna were at the ringside. We rose, took a few bows, and climbed into the ring. We wound up flat on our backs. They had forgotten to stop the fights. Hope said this was the first time he had ever been hit before he said anything.

Bob looked at home in the ring. In a way he is a middleweight champion. He has a lot of weight around the middle. We got out of the ring and went back to sit down. The main event of the evening started. And what a fight that was—kicking, gouging, name-calling, hair-pulling, and foul blows galore. At last I admitted I was in the wrong seat.

Of course pugilistic combat hardly interests me. I never could see much in fights.

The other fellow always closed my eyes.

As we left the crowd gave us a tremendous ovation. I only wish I could have brought it home with me, but it wouldn't fit in my suitcase.

That night I dreamed I was fighting for championship of the world. My opponent was Battling Bob Hope, the Cleveland Clouter. As he climbed through the ropes, I was awe-struck by his brilliant polka-dot boxing trunks. Holding them up was a gold championship belt with his eyes peering over it! I thought, what an underhand thing to do, as I pulled my own belt tighter around my neck.

As the gong sounded for the first round, we both crept slowly toward the center of the ring, where our seconds stopped pushing us and got out of the ring. Battling Bob shot out a vicious left. I shot out my vicious chin and blocked it. He crossed with a right, and I tried to lift my fists to stop it, but I couldn't. Those anvils in my gloves were too heavy.

Toe to toe we stood there slugging it out. I grinned at him. He gnashed his teeth at me and bit off the buckle of his belt. Finally, I landed a solid blow just below his ear. Battling Bob went down, and K. O. Colonna woke up.

As I came out of my dream, I realized that Hope had been dreaming along the same lines. He was sitting on the floor, holding his chin, and screaming, "Foul! Foul!"

Seeing it was already daylight, I dressed and sauntered down to the ocean.

While standing on the docks I noticed a group of little native boys diving for pennies. I spent a good hour tossing coins to them, but the boys complained. They said I wasn't supposed to dive in after them.

The divers taught me a way to increase my earnings. The trick was to pick a coin off the bottom of the bay, put it in my mouth, and go after another. I soon accumulated quite an amount. When I went home for lunch Hope, with his customary greeting, tugged at my mustache. He hit the jackpot!

That afternoon we went out to the ball park. We had heard that Joe DiMaggio was supposed to play. But when we arrived at the park, Joe didn't show up. Hope guessed DiMaggio didn't come because he was tired of hitting coconuts. Imagine belting out a home run and getting a milk bath at the same time!

The fellows told us that once while they were playing ball a Jap plane came over and strafed the field. The center fielder made the greatest play in baseball. He caught a fly ball and dug himself a fox hole at the same time. He just sat there and tagged all the base runners out one by one as they came rushing into the fox hole.

During the ball game, one of the batters hit a pop fly into the stands. It dropped right on my head. I can safely say this was the first time a foul ball ever hit a foul ball.

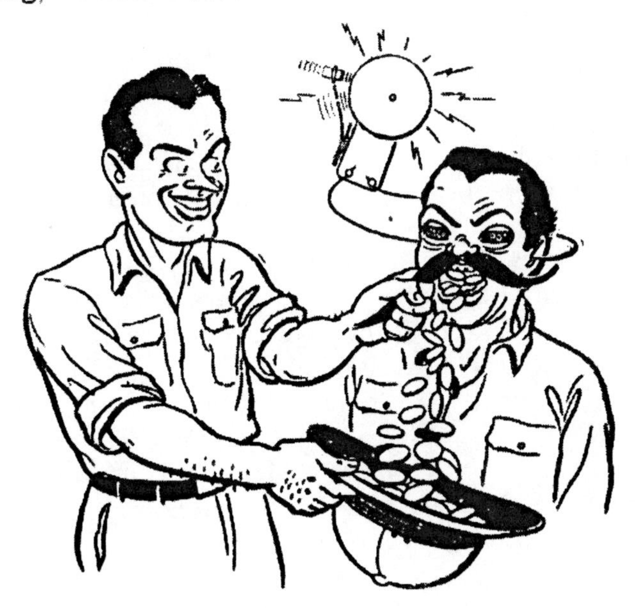

| U. S. O. UNIT | DATE | PLACE | AUDIENCE |
|---|---|---|---|
| *#130* | *July 13* | *Navy Yard* | *20,000* |

**A SHOW FOR THE CIVILIAN WORKERS**

**or**

**THEY WERE RIVETED TO THE SPOT**

TODAY we entertained the civilian workers in the military plants on the island. The audience was made up of Americans imported from the states as well as Hawaiians. These Hawaiians have a very colorful language. When I was entering the plant, a number of native workers greeted me with shouts of, "Kapu! Kapu!"

I replied, "Gesundheit!"

A Kamaaina, (an old-timer to us hep Hawaiians) tapped me on the shoulder and asked, "Do you realize what those workers are saying to you?"

"No," I said.

"Kapu means 'keep out,' or 'no trespassing,' or—'scram, jerk'!"

I thought my life in Hawaii would be smoother if I could say something in their language besides "Scram, jerk." I asked him to tell me something nice to say, and he suggested "Mele Kla̓kimaka." This is their way of saying Merry Christmas. Since this was only July the thirteenth, I figured I'd have a long wait before I could say anything nice to a Hawaiian.

The Hawaiians have a curious way of accentuating their expressions. For instance, "Meha" means lonely. "Mehameha" means very lonely. "Mehamehameha" means even your best friends won't tell you.

I was interrupted in my language lesson by Hope who came rushing out to tell me that our show had already started. I asked him if everything was going "Maikai," which means good. He said it was my turn to go on, which means bad.

As I went out on the stage a roar went up. It didn't upset me in the least. I had been on stages that were mined before.

While I was singing "I Love Life," a few of the workers walked out. My voice made them homesick for their rivet guns.

Patty Thomas really went over. The way she does the rhumba is the hottest thing this side of the Bethlehem Steel Company. Even the air conditioning in the plant was smoking.

When we were through, the hospitable Hawaiians put on a show for us. They put on a program of native dances and music. The dances were great. We never got around to listening to the music. Ten Hawaiian girls who worked at the plant came out in native costumes and did the hula hula. Well, what do you know! A swing shift in grass skirts! I feel that I should remark right here that I didn't flirt with any of the hula girls. Too shaky a proposition.

Hope described the hula hula with uncanny accuracy. He said, "The front of you stands still while the back of you makes like a jeep."

The next number was the "Hawaiian War Chant." It's a direct steal from the number Tommy Dorsey made famous.

After that a couple of native girls came back and danced some more hula hula. I felt very witty for a moment and turned to Hope. "What are they doing? Reducing?"

Hope snapped, "Yeah, reducing my resistance."

Two soldiers sitting in the audience watched the dancing with much interest. One turned to the other and said, "Gee! why can't the Army make its rotation system work like that?"

When their show was over I asked one of the hula girls to dance with me, but she refused. She said the sparks coming out of my nose might ignite her gra.s skirt. What a silly thing to say! I just laughed and put out the brush fire in my mustache.

As I lay in my bed that night I realized that the dances we had seen that day made quite an impression on me. I was still cross-eyed!

| U. S. O. UNIT | PLACE | AUDIENCE |
|---|---|---|
| *#130* | *Unit Jungle Training Center* | *7,000* |
| DATE | *Fort Hase* | *5,000* |
| *July 15* | *Tripler Hospital* | *2,000* |

### JUNGLE CAMOUFLAGE
### or
### WOODSMAN SPARE THAT TREE— IT'S ME!

WHEN Hope told us we were going to visit the Jungle Training center I was thrilled.

We rode there in a jeep called "Stardust." It was a very rugged ride. I called it everything but "Stardust." We bounced along for about four choruses. They were the sorest choruses I've ever known.

When we arrived all the G. I.'s were dressed in jungle camouflage suits. You couldn't tell where they began and the scenery ended. I remarked to Col. Safferin, the commanding officer, that I thought it would be easier to do it the other way around. Instead of making the men look like trees, make the trees look like men.

The Colonel, "You have a brilliant idea there. Now, I want you to promise me not to tell anyone. They might steal it."

He suggested we don the camouflage suits ourselves. What a transformation. We all looked like trees, that is with the exception of Barney Dean. With his bald head he resembled a sun-flower. Hope took one look at me in my odd get-up and said, "It's the first time I've ever seen a bush wearing a bush."

Incidentally Hope standing there in that suit with his nose pointing out looked just like a great oak with a great poke.

We all got in the spirit of the thing. Even Frances and Patty dressed up as trees. I couldn't see the point to that. They couldn't improve on the limbs they already had. When the girls appeared on the scene a chorus went up from the trees, "Hey look, Fellas! Babes in the woods!" They nearly started a forest fire.

As I stood there clad in my leafy garments, I softly repeated to myself:

"I think that I shall never see
A poem lovely as a tree."

Hope said, "If Joyce Kilmer could see you now, he'd tear up his poem!"

As we watched the men go through the rugged obstacle course under a barrage of live ammunition, Colonel Safferin asked me if I'd like to join them.

I said, "Live ammunition might be all right for them, but I prefer a live Colonna."

The fellows put on demonstrations at various obstacles at the course. I remember in particular a twenty-foot stream. The only way to get to the other side was to swing across on a vine. I decided I'd give it a try. It happened to be my stupid time in the afternoon. I ran, grabbed the vine and leaped into the air a la Tarzan. I landed in the middle of the stream a la Colonna. Even at that it was easier to cross on that vine in Oahu than it was to cross Sunset and Vine in Hollywood.

Hope reminded me that I'd forgotten to put down the flaps on my mustache and that's why I ground looped. As I started to float down stream Hope yelled to me to start swimming. I said I didn't know how. He said, "Now's a good time to learn!"

Finally somebody threw me a life jacket. I tossed it back. I demanded a single-breasted model. The next thing I heard was a terrific splash. Hope had come to my rescue. With a jerk he pulled me out of the water. I don't remember what the jerk's name was.

After wringing out my mustache I turned to him and murmured gratefully, "Thanks, Hope. What made you risk your life to save me?"

Bob smiled tenderly at me. "You were wearing my wrist watch."

But Bob's joshing manner didn't conceal his real feeling toward me. It's been that way between us ever since. He still won't let me wear his wrist watch.

It was time for us to move on. We bid adieu to the men on the obstacle—but they outbid us, so we went away without the obstacle.

At one spot where the small-arms fire was being explained, Hope was invited to fire the light machinegun. Hope said he had seen Clark Gable fire a machinegun from the hip in a movie.

"If Gable can do it, I can. I've got more hip than he has."

Hope grabbed the gun and fired three times from his hip. The instructor told him he'd better stop.

"Aw, no," Hope said, "I'm not tired."

The instructor said, "Maybe you're not tired, but the men who keep picking you up are worn out."

Inspired by Hope's performance I seized the machinegun. I dropped the machinegun. Why didn't somebody tell me the barrel was hot? I picked up the machinegun, sighted the target, fired a burst, and missed. Took a few steps forward, fired a burst, missed. Forward, burst, missed! Forward, burst, missed! Monotonous, isn't it? Closer still, fired, missed!

The instructor yelled to me, "Got news for you. You'll never hit that target now. It's behind you."

A little thing like that couldn't discourage

an old trick shot rifleman like Colonna. I took out a mirror, lined up the target, and fired. Egad! Seven years bad luck! And I was only on the fourth year of my previous seven.

This was the first gun to give me any trouble. All my life I have been a great lover of firearms. When I was a small lad my father got a rifle for me—but my mother stopped him before he could draw a bead on me.

The gun was given to me on my next birthday. I spent my youth tracking and hunting, hunting and tracking. There was nothing I wouldn't track. Many times I was spanked for tracking mud through the house. But I did bag a few prize specimens. The wall over the fireplace was covered with my trophies: the top of an old tomato can, part of the side of a barn door (which I missed), and a turkey's tail feathers (I could have sworn it was an Indian).

So you can understand how disappointed I was at not being able to handle a simple light machinegun there in the training center. I must confess my temper got the better of me. I kicked the machinegun. I kicked it again. And again. And again. And again. Finally I stopped. I had run out of toes!

I looked up and saw that the gang had moved on to the next station. An instructor was giving them a lecture on Ju-jitsu and jungle fighting. When I arrived, Hope was wrestling with a two-hundred-and-fifty-pound moving mountain with Sergeant stripes on his sleeves. They rolled over the ground. They struggled back and forth, even back and fifth. Hope was handling this two-hundred-and-fifty-pounder as if his hands and feet were tied. They were! Finally they called the match a draw. Then they drew Hope out of the ground. He looked just like a tube of Pepsodent after the last squeeze.

With blood in his eye the Sergeant turned to me. "Hey, Tumbleweed! How about exchanging a few holds?"

I looked at him and grinned. "What have I got to lose?"

I soon found out.

The Sergeant explained that there were no rules in hand-to-hand combat. He said you could pick, punch, gouge, strangle. Anything goes. I went!

I didn't get far away before my pride returned. Something made me go back and face it. It was the Sergeant's hand around my throat. He tried a few holds on me and asked me if they hurt. I never cried out once. It's hard to do when you're unconscious. Since that tussle my vertebrae have never seen each other since.

After completing the course the instructor handed me an engraved certificate. I was qualified to enter the hospital immediately.

| U. S. O. UNIT | DATE | PLACE | AUDIENCE |
|---|---|---|---|
| *#130* | *July 17* | *Kauai* | *15,000* |

## OFF TO KAUAI
## or
## KAUAI NOT?

WE hit the road again. It was the only thing we weren't afraid to hit. Today we were booked to exhibit our talents to the Yanks on Kauai. This was the most northerly of the Hawaiian group. Kauai rhymes with Hawaii. That's why they put it so far away. (Now that you can pronounce Kauai, go back and read the chapter title again.)

The sun was just rising when we awoke that morning. Ah! Dawn was a lovely sight! Too bad she had a boy friend. I've never been able to get up with the sun. I guess it's because I can't sleep that high. However, I am a strong advocate of clean living. I get up in the morning, jump out of bed, fall right on my face! In my more vigorous days I used to run around the block three times every day. I finally had to give it up. My little boy wanted his block back.

These reflections were interrupted by little Barney Dean, who came running in, in a huff. It didn't fit him too well. Too long in the sleeves. It seems that during the night a moth had devoured his pants. This didn't anger Barney as much as the note the moth left. He showed it to me.

"Thanks for the hors d'oeuvres, but next time I'd appreciate a full course meal." If you don't think this actually happened, please don't tell other people.

When we had all been seated on the plane, it took off for Kauai. Once again as Oahu faded into the distance, I got that same old feeling of leaving something behind—my stomach!

We landed in Kauai. It was a veritable tropical garden spot. There were trees and flowers all around our plane. The pilot had overshot the airstrip.

The fellows who came to greet us told me that Kauai was truly a Paradise—a Garden of Eden.

Before I knew it, I was shouting, "Well, what are we waiting for? Where's Eve?"

My feelings often take possession of me like this. Their lease allows them to.

It didn't take us long to discover that the men on this island suffered from the one ailment army and navy medicine can't cure—homesickness. But I fixed that. After one look at me, they weren't homesick anymore—just sick.

Hope had a more practical method for driving away their gloom. He slanted the jokes in his monologue at their respective home states.

For instance, for the boys from California, he said, "The way things grow out in California! Why only last week I planted a little bit of a tree, and already the squirrels have condemned it. Everything in California grows fast. When the stork delivers a baby, he throws in a package of blue blades free."

And for the fellows from Florida:

"And are they hospitable in Florida—if you watch what you say. I walked into a fruit store and asked for a dozen Sunkist oranges. That's all I remember."

For the G.I.'s from below the Mason and Dixon line, Hope threw in:

"I like Georgia. What a country! Peaches as far as the eye can see. Once in a while one of them looks back. I walked up to one of those Georgia peaches, looked her over carefully, and I said, 'Baby, are you a freestone?' She said, 'No, and I'm not a clingstone either, so don't expect me to nectarine!'"

Hope pulled a gag about every state in the Union, but he couldn't say anything about my state. He had no jokes about unconsciousness.

After the show they served us a dinner consisting solely of K rations. For dessert I ate the can it came in. Now I know why they put K rations in cans. The cans take away the taste of the K rations. After dinner the commanding officer came up to me and said, "Didn't you enjoy your dinner?"

"Why certainly," I said, "why do you ask?"

He pointed to my plate, "You haven't eaten the label."

I was ashamed of myself. It was the brightest green label I have ever seen on any can. My mother always told me that I should eat my greens.

After dinner we joined the men in a game of poker. Hope, by the way, had a wonderful definition of a poker game. He called it, "Chips that pass in the night."

For those of you who are not familiar with poker, the sport of Kings and Queens, I would like to give you a few pointers on the game. Poker is a game where you lay down some money, pick up five cards, lay down some more money, look at your cards, lay down your cards, and then *you* go lay down.

One of the best hands in poker is four aces. Of course, some people have held five aces. Of course, they're dead. Of course. It's apparent, the longer you play poker, the quicker you get broker.

However, I enjoyed playing poker that night on Kauai. It was a very warm night, but as the game progressed it became cooler. I couldn't understand the reason for this until I discovered I had lost my shirt. Hope just sat there and laughed at me as he pulled his underwear closer around him. Tony Romano didn't do so well either. All he was wearing was a G-string from his guitar.

After we'd lost all our money at the poker game, Hope suggested we turn in. He said he was drowsy.

"That's us," I replied, "a great team—Drowsy and Lousy."

I lay down on my Army cot, but I couldn't sleep. The guy who invented the word "uncomfortable" was lying on one of those cots when he thought of it. After a while I decided to try sleeping on the ground. There was a spring running through the ground, which is more than I can say for the cot. I slept in a pup tent that night, but all night long the pup kept asking me to move over.

I decided to get up and go outside for awhile. There I found Tony Romano.

He asked me if I had insomnia.

I said, "No, is he missing?"

Tony told me that if I couldn't sleep the best way to overcome it was to lie down, close my eyes, and start counting sheep.

My problem solved! Joyously I returned to my cot. When I had counted my 10,953rd sheep (including the black ones) it happened! It was morning!

Since then I have come to the conclusion that there is just one sure cure for insomnia: Hit yourself over the head with a mallet.

| U. S. O. UNIT | DATE | PLACE | AUDIENCE |
|---|---|---|---|
| *#130* | *July 20* | *Christmas Island* | *650* |

### CHRISTMAS ISLAND
### or
### THIS WILL TEACH YOU NOT TO HANG YOUR STOCKINGS UP!

AFTER nine days on the Hawaiian Islands, we were scheduled for a long jump to the south.

I was very excited about our coming trip. I started packing with fervor. Hope told me we were going into the war zone. I started unpacking with fervor.

Tony Romano's trunk was too full. He asked me to come over and help him close it. We struggled for an hour, but it was no use. I finally told him he'd have to take that native girl out of there.

Tony was very embarrassed. He said he couldn't imagine how that beautiful girl got there. But I could imagine. In fact, I spent a delectable two hours trying to get one into my trunk.

I rushed down to the lobby and kissed the hotel manager goodbye. Maybe you think this is a very silly custom. Ah! but you don't know what a gorgeous girl that hotel manager was!

In due time we arrived at the airport. I thought to myself: If I go on flying much longer, I'll be able to do it without a plane.

Lieutenant General C. Richardson, commanding general of the Hawaiian Defense Sector, provided our transportation. The plane was a special Liberator bomber gone civilian. Appropriately named "Seventh Heaven," it was completely furnished. There was an ice box where the bombs used to be. It seemed strange to look through the Norden Bomb Sight and see two pickles and a hunk of salami. A piece of apple pie was coming in at "twelve o'clock." I couldn't make up my mind which I liked better, the ice box or the comfortably upholstered chairs. After making several trips back and forth, I decided I preferred an overstuffed Colonna to an overstuffed chair. That plane was really a home in the sky!

A group of officers representing General Richardson was down to see us off. We shook hands all around, and said we'd enjoyed our nine-day visit, and were sorry to leave. They said they were even sorrier than we were—they wished we had left sooner. I didn't take these cracks seriously. It was merely good-natured banter. After we made a few parting jokes, however, they picked us up bodily and threw us on the plane.

Our engines were warmed up, the chocks pulled out from in front of the wheels, and down the airstrip we rolled for a takeoff.

We were airborne again. It has always been a source of amazement to me that a huge, heavy thing like a bomber can float in the air. Why, I can't even lift it with my two hands. Hope has frequently explained to me that planes are sustained in the air by the principles of aerodynamics. Maybe so. But I have carefully scrutinized the wings, the fuselage, and the landing gear, and I have one question to ask. Where are these principles of aerodynamics attached? Having disposed of the traditional theory of flight, I come to my own far more satisfactory explanation: airplanes stay up in the air for the same reason that birds, bats, and bees do. They like it there! Read this over a few times, and if you are not sufficiently confused, read it over backwards. It is the Colonna Formula for Aeronautical Propulsion in a nut shell. Perhaps by now you are beginning to doubt my sanity. After all, what did you *expect* to find in a nut shell?

I was aroused from my mathematical calculations by the co-pilot. He told me we were aiming for Christmas Island, a bit of rock fifteen hundred miles south of Hawaii. However, I wasn't worried. Our pilot was plenty sharp. Not only could he land the plane on a dime, but he could do it without breaking up the crap game. Fifteen hundred miles were nothing to him. We covered the distance before I could say Jack Robinson in Turkish.

So we came to Christmas Island. It looked like the Locust Plague had beat us to it. Bare and desolate, Christmas Island is practically what was left over after the world was made.

When he first saw this place, Hope remarked, "Who designed this place? Bela Lugosi?"

The rest of us agreed.

He added, "This is just the spot to check your old nightmares."

Hope was right.

The island is saturated with blister bugs and land crabs. The crabs will pinch you anywhere they can get a hold. I discovered that fact when I sat down on one of them. Chemical tests show that the water surrounding the island contains a small percentage of alcohol. This might be the reason why the crabs walk sideways. If it isn't the reason, you think of one.

Blister bugs, on the other hand, are generally found on the other hand. Once these bugs land on you, they start digging into your skin. They're the bulldozers of the insect world. The theme song of the island is "I've Got You Under My Skin." One of these bugs dug into me so far he struck oil. This might require some explanation, so I will pass it off by saying that my last transfusion was given to me by a filling station attendant. As is to be expected this has considerably altered my blood pressure. I now carry thirty-two pounds in each leg.

I wondered why they called these insects "blister bugs." You must never, never, never slap a blister bug while it's on your person. When crushed they spray you with their poison and up pops a blister.

I was frantic. There had to be some way to remove the blister bugs from my arms and legs.

I said to myself, "Colonna, use your head!"

It didn't work out. They bit just as hard there.

I decided to use the same tactics I had developed to combat the insects in my victory garden at home. I would get my spray gun, spray the bugs well, then spray myself. Then the bugs would sit around nibbling at my vegetables while waiting for me to come to.

Never will I forget the experience I had with a horse fly. For days I shadowed him. Finally my supreme moment arrived! I saw him there. Sitting calmly. Not twitching a twitch. I picked up a heavy board, crept up behind him, and let him have it. Wham!

That episode broke my leg. The horse fly had been roosting on a horse.

So, with this ill luck in my fight to exterminate the bugs, you can see why my victory garden wound up in total defeat.

I came to the conclusion that the only way to handle blister bugs was to ignore them. Was I going to let a little bug worry me? Of course not! And besides that suit of armor only set me back twenty bucks.

In an effort to forget about the blister bugs, we went out to the island ball park. One thing we learned in traveling throughout these islands was that baseball was the G.I.'s favorite sport. After the landing forces have taken the place, the first thing the Seabees build is the airstrip, the second is a baseball diamond.

For the benefit of you who do not know what baseball is—count me in. Nevertheless, I managed to secure a copy of Spaulding's Baseball Guide. They give one away free with every purchase. I bought a tennis court and a swimming pool. They'd been so nice to me, I didn't want to walk out of the store without buying something.

I studied the book and here are some facts and figures. Figures: take Patty Thomas—no, we'd better go back to facts. Facts: two men are responsible for the invention of our national pastime. Colonel Abner Doubleday thought of the idea in 1839, and Professor Gerard Colonna had the same idea exactly one hundred years later. I am still suing Abner for plagiarism.

But let's leave the specific and get back to the Pacific. When we arrived at the Christmas Island ball park, the fellows asked Frances to be field umpire. She took her position right next to the short-stop. Immediately the team adopted a most unusual fielding set-up—nine short-stops!

After a few innings one of the managers asked Patty Thomas if she would like to pitch a little. She slapped his face before Hope had time to explain that he was referring to baseball. I'm still not convinced he was.

The leading batter of the team was the first to face Patty. He was helpless. He had never before seen anyone throw an inside and outside curve at the same time.

Hope also pitched for a while. Hope is a very fine ball player. You've heard of a no-hit, no-run game? Well, Hope once pitched a no-hit, no-run, no-game—rain! For this feat he was elected the most valuable player in the Girls' Softball League.

I taught Hope everything he knows about baseball. It was Colonna who taught him to hit, bunt, and steal bases. And it was Colonna who paid the fine when he wouldn't put them back.

All in all, we had a lot of fun entertaining and playing baseball with the fellows, but when I tramped to the plane through a mass of land crabs and blister bugs, Christmas Island reminded me of Thanksgiving. I was so thankful to leave it.

| U. S. O. UNIT | DATE | PLACE | AUDIENCE |
|---|---|---|---|
| *#130* | *July 21* | *Canton* | *1,000* |

**SOUTHWEST HO!**
**or**
**A TREE GROWS IN CANTON**

CANTON Island was next.

We flew southeast crossing the equator. According to tradition when you cross the equator for the first time, you're supposed to have your head shaved. With this in mind, the co-pilot started after Barney Dean, then took a look at his bald scalp and muttered disappointedly, "How do you like that. This guy came prepared for everything!"

Next they started for me. They planned the most horrible things they could do to my appearance. I looked them right in the eye and they stopped in their tracks. What they had in mind would have only improved my looks.

The plane finally came to rest on Canton Island. It is not exactly what you'd call heavily wooded. Sort of a purgatory for dogs. Just one tree.

The men on this island were plenty proud of the tree. They called it "Coconut Grove." The cover charge there was a dive into the closest fox hole.

There were many theories current around the island to account for the presence of this lone tree. One was that this was the Tree that grew in Brooklyn trying to get away from it all. Another was that the seed had been planted upside down in Florida and the tree had come through the wrong way. Sort of a coconut Corrigan.

After studying the situation carefully, I came to the conclusion that they were all wrong. It wasn't a tree at all. Just a mirage somebody saw in Peoria, Illinois and it got too shady and had to leave town. If you follow me, tell me where we are because I'm lost.

But what a crossroads this tiny Pacific island is! Planes keep swooping down and taking off in constant procession.

Hope watched them for a while and then said, "It reminds me of Crosby's roof when the storks start dropping their bundles."

I said, "No kidding?"

He shook his head. "Where Crosby's concerned there's plenty of kidding."

As we sauntered around the island I was told there used to be cannibals living here. Instead of saying, "What's cooking?" they used to say, "Is it anybody we know?"

One of the famous cannibal dishes on this island was their quick lunch. They called it a manburger.

All this talk of food made me hungry. I thought maybe Hope could help me. I looked at him, but he took my knife away from me and said there were limits to our friendship. We strolled over to the enlisted men's mess.

As we walked through the mess hall I noticed that the fellows really relished their food. It took plenty of relish.

As I walked into the kitchen, the Mess Sergeant came forward to greet me, his face wreathed in smiles. "Well, if it isn't Professor Colonna!"

I nodded. "If it isn't, I've been living a lie."

The Sergeant said, "I've been saving something special for you."

"A steak?"

He shook his head.

"Ice cream?"

"Uh, uh, now you're getting cold."

Before I knew it, I discovered a bushel basket of potatoes in my lap.

"Peel these," the Sergeant snarled.

"What'sa matter? Ya crazy or somethin'? You'll *never* get me to peel any potatoes."

The Sergeant raised his arm. He said, "Take a look at that muscle."

"I don't have time to look," I said, "I'm very busy peeling potatoes."

By the time I had peeled three bushels, I had muscles bigger than his. I stood up, dumped the potatoes in his lap, and went home.

Our quarters on the island were huts of the south sea type just like you see in the movies, with one trifling difference. Dorothy Lamour isn't inside. These huts look like pup tents wearing grass skirts.

There's only one thing wrong with this type of hut. One of the divisions had a goat for a mascot and it literally ate them out of house and home.

Also, one of the officers was resting in his hut one evening. He lit a cigarette and inhaled his front room.

After our trip and all the shows we gave, those huts were like the Ritz Carlton to us. I can safely make this statement since I've never stayed at the Ritz Carlton.

Just to make sure I would sleep well, I decided to pace the floor for a while. This proved futile. The floor set too fast a pace.

I jumped into bed, turned over on my side, and slept like a log. In fact, in the morning they had to yell "Timberrrrrrrr" to get me out of bed.

| U. S. O. UNIT | DATE | PLACE | AUDIENCE |
|---|---|---|---|
| *#130* | *July 23* | *Tarawa* | *3,000* |

### OUR SHOW AT TARAWA
### or
### THE PLEASURE WAS ALL OURS

WE arrived at Tarawa about one year after the Marines made it possible for people like us to arrive at Tarawa.

A Navy captain met the plane. He welcomed us to the island and said, "I am P. E. Gillespie, Captain, U. S. N."

Hope introduced himself, "I am Bob Hope, Comedian, U. S. O."

I put in, "I am Jerry Colonna, Professor, take it or leave it!"

He left it!

Bob told me Captain Gillespie was a very important guy in the Navy. He said, "Look at the scrambled eggs on his cap."

I said, "Hope, don't be catty. You've got scrambled eggs on your tie!"

The Captain showed us all around the island. He pointed out the spots where the scars of the famous battle hadn't yet healed. Later he showed us where we were to stay. We were quartered near the native village. We had no complaints. It was much better than being drawn and quartered.

For the past two or three days I had been suffering from a little gum trouble in my front teeth. Hope tried to soothe me by reading a few Pepsodent commercials. Now I know why they won't let him read them on the radio. Captain Gillespie suggested I see Lieutenant Kelly, U.S.N., the local dentist. The moment he mentioned the word dentist, I mentioned I had never felt better in all my life. The pain immediately shot to my right ear. Captain Gillespie was dragging me to the dentist. I said I would go peacefully and Captain Gillespie said, "All right." I walked four steps before I realized he hadn't let go of my ear. Barney Dean went along with me. He had nothing to do that afternoon, so he thought he'd pass the time of day by having his teeth cleaned.

It was a rustic dental office. A bamboo hut with a thatched roof. It looked something like my mouth when I'm singing "Chloe." Inside was a big comfortable dentist chair fully equipped with bowl, head rest, and straight jacket. I looked up at the Lieutenant, "Doctor," I said, "I'm having a little trouble with my gums in front here, nothing serious. I thought maybe a little dab of something—"

"Open your mouth," he said, and grabbed an instrument that looked like a small bulldozer.

Lieutenant Kelly looked at Barney Dean, who was blushing at the medical journal. He patted me on the shoulder and said, "Relax. You don't want to disgrace yourself in front of your son."

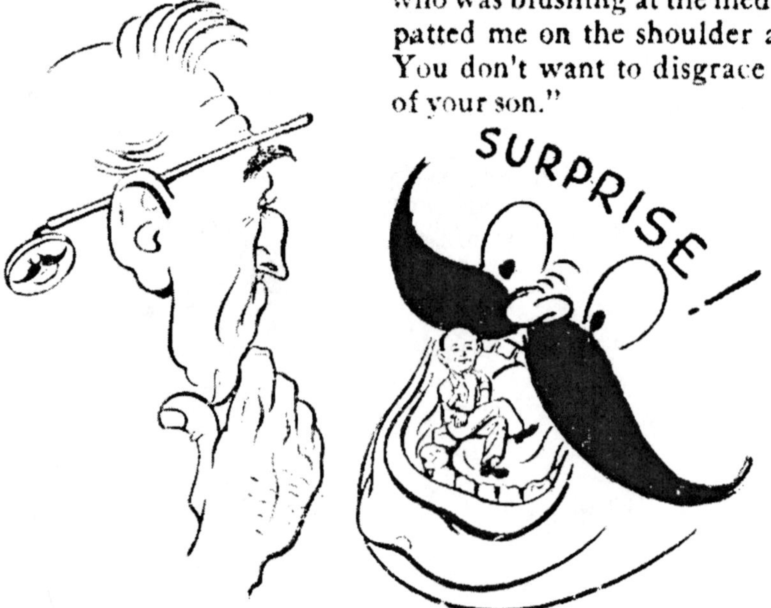

*Say "Tarawa"!*

I told him Barney Dean was too old to be my son even though he did have a head that looked like a new-born baby. He just laughed and asked Barney to hand him his pliers.

Quickly I explained, "The gums, Doctor, nothing serious," pointing to the spot in front with my forefinger, "maybe a little dab—" It was no use, he was already fighting his way through my underbrush and peering into my mouth. Barney also was curiously looking inside my mouth. The doctor told him he would have to go sit down. He couldn't work with somebody sitting on one of my molars.

Something caught the doctor's attention. He said, "Has this wisdom tooth been giving you any trouble lately?"

"No, and it hasn't been giving me any wisdom either."

"I think it will have to come out."

"Please, doctor, the gums. Maybe—"

"I agree with you," he said. "There's nothing seriously wrong with the gums, but that wisdom tooth, tch! tch! tch!"

"Maybe you're too busy. I'll come back tomorrow."

"I am pretty busy, but I think I can spare the time to pull that one wisdom tooth."

By this time his knee was on my chest.

There was a gleam in the doctor's eye. "Wait until I write to my wife and tell her I have a tooth out of Professor Colonna's mouth."

I told him if he was looking for souvenirs, I would gladly give him my watch.

Before I knew it he had given me a shot of novocaine. I felt more wide awake than I had ever felt in my life.

"Now," the doctor said, "say 'Tarawa'."

I did. The tooth popped out between "Tar" and "Awa."

He held my tooth aloft in triumph and looked over at Barney Dean. Barney was creeping toward the door.

The doctor called after him, "Just a minute, young man. Didn't you want me to clean your teeth?"

Barney said, "I want them cleaned, not cleaned out." And kept right on moving.

"I don't know what you fellows are so scared about," Lieutenant Kelly said. "I've never lost a man yet."

"Maybe not," I replied, "but I'll bet the men have lost a lot of teeth!" (And I'll bet he saved a lot too.) Lieutenant Kelly is a swell fellow, and a wonderful dentist. (He didn't charge me anything for pulling that tooth.)

The next day the whole troupe had lunch at Captain Gillespie's quarters. The food was fit for a king. The king never showed up, so we ate it.

At lunch we met Vice-Admiral Jones. He had been on the Battleship U.S.S. Maryland, which had done a lot of fighting in the battle for Tarawa. Admiral Jones was very helpful. He reorganized the schedule of our tour. We had planned on going directly to Guadalcanal, but he suggested we start at Eniwetok at the top of this group of islands and work our way down to Guadalcanal. In this way we would visit Tarawa again. The Admiral said this would be a much easier route to take, and besides, he would get to see our show twice. Hope told him that if he could stand the battle of Tarawa, he could stand to see our show twice.

Admiral Jones was in the audience that afternoon when we did our show. I guess he enjoyed it because he didn't change our route again—to Siberia.

The whole gang went over great that afternoon. I sang "The Road To Mandalay" like my bridge was washed out. I quickly followed with "Conchita." I wasn't giving them any time to think it over.

After the performance a corporal asked me if I had ever studied with Professor Simpson. I said I hadn't. I had never heard of him.

The corporal explained, "He's the champion hog-caller in the Ozarks."

Imagine! That was the first time anyone ever had the nerve to compare my voice to a hog-caller. Everyone else compared it to the hogs. But the hogs resented it.

We all retired early that evening. Just as I was turning in, Lieutenant Kelly dropped in on me to tell me he had seen the show that afternoon. I asked the doctor what he thought of my singing.

He said he wished he had left my wisdom tooth alone and taken out my tonsils.

| U. S. O. UNIT | DATE | PLACE | AUDIENCE |
|---|---|---|---|
| *#130* | *July 26* | *Eniwetok* | *10,500* |

**WE MEET A HOLLYWOOD SAILOR**
**or**
**HENRY MAKES OUR HEARTS GROW FONDA**

AGAIN the course of the "Seventh Heaven" was to the Northwest. This time our destination was Eniwetok.

We gave two shows today and packed them in. Our show's getting to be more like a minstrel show every day. The sun is giving us the right makeup for minstrels. In fact, we've been getting Amos and Andy's fan mail by mistake. You should have seen Barney's head. He had such a deep mahogany tan, we varnished him and sold him to the natives as a bridge lamp. Hope really had a suntan. He looked at himself in the mirror and said, "My eyes look like a pair of dice on an ebony floor."

At Eniwetok it was like old home week. We ran into Lieutenant, J.G., Henry Fonda. To the Navy J.G. means Junior Grade. But to Frances and Patty it meant Just Grand! Henry was appearing with Uncle Sam's Navy by courtesy of Twentieth-Century Fox. He was an aide to Vice-Admiral Hoover, the Darryl Zanuck of the island.

Hope and Henry chatted about their experiences in the movies. Hope asked him how it felt to kiss Gene Tierney.

"I get about the same thing out of it you get when you kiss Dorothy Lamour."

"You mean you get slapped every time too?"

Hearing them talk reminded me of the time I came to Hollywood.

I remember my first break in pictures—CUT!

Then there was the time I was a producer.

Then there was the time I co-starred with Bette Davis.

Then there was the time I caught myself dreaming. Right now!

If Hope hadn't awakened me, who knows? I might have gotten the Academy Award. It was such a nice day, he had decided I should take a little walk around the island. This might seem silly to you, but I am always kind to little walks.

These islands have more animals and bugs per square foot than there are people back home trying to find out Who Threw That Coconut. Strolling around Eniwetok, you certainly get to know "Who's Who in the Zoo."

I woke up one morning, rolled over, and there was a boa constrictor curled up beside me on the pillow. I yawned and said, "Don't get up, dear, I'll make the coffee this morning."

I had already put the pot on to boil before I realized that the snake was a perfect stranger to me. Three hours later I began to calm down a little, but that was after they had given me the shot in the arm.

As I returned from my walk I came across

a soldier crooning sweet nothings to the moon. Those men really got lonesome out there. This fellow spent two hours every night trying to date his echo—just to keep in practice.

This seemed like a good idea to me, so I sat down beside the soldier and tossed a few sugary phrases into the breeze. My echo broke off our engagement.

So ended a typical day on Eniwetok.

Before we boarded the plane to fly to Kwajelein I was surrounded by thousands of G. I.'s. Hope was amazed at my popularity. He never found out that the captain had asked me to distribute their pay. I enjoyed giving the fellows their money. I was so thrilled I gave away twenty dollars of my own money. I would be very grateful to hear from the fellow who got it. He'll know it's my money by the mustache on Washington's face.

| U. S. O. UNIT | DATE | PLACE | AUDIENCE |
|---|---|---|---|
| *#130* | *July 28* | *Kwajelein* | *13,000* |

**THE MOSQUITO NETWORK**
**or**
**N.B.C. WITH D.D.T.**

I WOKE up with a start this morning. Only my left eye was open! But my fears were calmed when I realized that all night I had been only half asleep. My right eye was tired and turned in early, but my left eye felt quite gay and decided to make a night of it. Feeling much better after this revelation, I rushed off to hop the plane for Kwajelein.

Kwajelein, translated from the ancient Polynesian to English, and then translated back to the the ancient Polynesian again, means—Kwajelein. This word brings back old memories to me. I first spelled it when I was in the third grade. Of course, at the time I was trying to spell "cat."

The island of Kwajelein is a beautiful place—from thirty thousand feet up. It looks like a diamond in the rough. But when you get down to the rough, it looks like somebody swiped the diamond.

When we landed the weather was unbearable.

I turned to Hope and remarked, "Egad! Isn't it hot and sticky!"

Hope said, "I wouldn't know. *I* wasn't hit with a casava melon."

I screamed, "This is sabotage!" Then I licked my face and said, "No, you're right. It's casava!" and walked right into a very powerful radio station operated by the Armed Forces Radio Service. It covers a large portion of the mid-Pacific area. It is heard as far as Saipan on one side and Guadalcanal on the other. Broadcasts of G.I. Journal, Mail Call, and Command Performance are relayed from here either by shortwave from the United States, or by transcription. They also broadcast the other big radio shows we hear at home, but without the commercial advertising.

To show you what effect the lack of product plugs has on the men, one soldier said to me, "I'm completely out of touch. I haven't heard a commercial in three years. Tell me, has Mirium gotten around to using Irium yet?"

The whole set-up is called "The Mosquito Network." They call it that because nobody ever found a mosquito net that works. It's sort of a N.B.C. with D.D.T.!

The Kwajelein station was set up under the jurisdiction of Colonel Tom Lewis. Colonel Lewis was one of the chief organizers of the "Mosquito Network" and a founder of the Armed Forces Radio Service. He is also the husband of Loretta Young. Egad! What one man can't pack into a lifetime.

Our next job was to make a transcription of our show to be used at places which due to military restrictions we weren't allowed to visit.

I stepped up to the mike and did a couple of numbers for the transcription. One thing about me, I don't get mike fright. Of course, the microphone gets a little squeamish.

The engineer came out of the control booth and said I was losing my modulation.

"I don't wonder," I said. "I've been on a diet for the past week."

As I stood there before the microphone I marveled at the mechanical wonder of radio transmission. I stand there and sing. It is my voice! But in a moment it undergoes a miraculous transformation. It enters a multitude of tiny holes no more than 3/16ths of an inch in diameter, goes down a long pipe to the floor, is carried along rubber sheathed wires to the amplifier, weaves in and out of audions, klystrons, condensers, and audio-transformers, and at last comes out of the loud-speaker. My voice! The same in every detail! All that work and no improvement!

| U. S. O. UNIT | DATE | PLACE | AUDIENCE |
|---|---|---|---|
| *#130* | *July 28* | *Makin* | *5,000* |

### ON THE MAKIN ROUTE
### or
### DELIVERING MILK TO THE JAPS

ON our way to Makin we flew high over Mili Island. It was part of the Marshalls still held by the Japs. We heard the Nips' anti-aircraft guns exploding below, but I didn't see any flak. In fact, it was impossible to see anything from underneath my chair. I wasn't frightened. I merely lost my head and was looking under the chair for it.

Barney Dean kept calling me "Fraidy Cat." I told him to shut up and get out of Tony's guitar.

Fortunately, there was no Jap air interception and we were too high for the flak to reach us. The pilot said there wasn't a chance in a million of us being hit. What a small number a million is!

To get even with the Japs for scaring the K-rations out of us, we rounded up some empty milk bottles and dropped them on the island. Going down they whistle just like falling bombs. I aimed most carefully and I'm sure I hit some one with my milk bottle. I'm still looking for a Jap with a Borden haircut.

The Nips reacted quickly to our homogenized bombing. Ten minutes later a carrier pigeon with slant eyes, landed on our wing with a note tied to its foot. It read: "Tomorrow please a pint of honorable coffee cream." It seems they were expecting the Marines for dinner.

On Makin we had a wonderful lunch with Captain Grant, U.S.N. The smartest thing a man can do on these islands is have lunch with a Navy Captain. Especially right after a supply ship has docked. On the plate before me was a thick piece of some strange meat. At first I didn't recognize it. Then I awakened—a steak! This was no ordinary porterhouse. It was more of a porter-skyscraper! Also in front of me was a glass of *fresh* milk, plates of fresh vegetables, mashed potatoes, cranberry sauce, French pastry and ice cream!

Frances took a long look at this display, sighed heavily, and said, "Remove the mirage and bring on the food."

The Captain assured her it was the real McCoy.

Hope said, "The Navy has a much better idea of K-rations than the Army has."

Patty Thomas exclaimed, "The food looks so good. I'm not even going to think of my figure!"

"It looks so good, *I'm* not even going to think of your figure," somebody said. It could have been me—I was thinking it.

Captain Grant asked me what I thought of the chow.

I gulped. "You mean to say we're eating dog meat?"

Hope just barked and went right on eating.

Frances explained that chow is a Navy term for food.

Was I embarrassed! A couple of other times I had been embarrassed. Once I bit my tongue in vexation. Another time I stubbed my toe in Pittsburgh!

Tony was so hungry, he stood in the middle of his steak and ate his way out. He is so thin, vitamins take him!

My appetite was ravenous! I tore through my food. Worcestershire sauce, cut, chew. Worcestershire sauce, cut, chew. Worcestershire sauce, cut — "Ouch!" — Egad! I had worked my way up to the Captain's hand!

The greatest treat was the chance to drink fresh milk again. We hadn't touched a drop since we left the states. Now we drank milk until the cows came home. Then we milked them and drank some more.

When we were through eating, I shook hands with Captain Grant and expressed my appreciation in a word: "Mooooooooooo!"

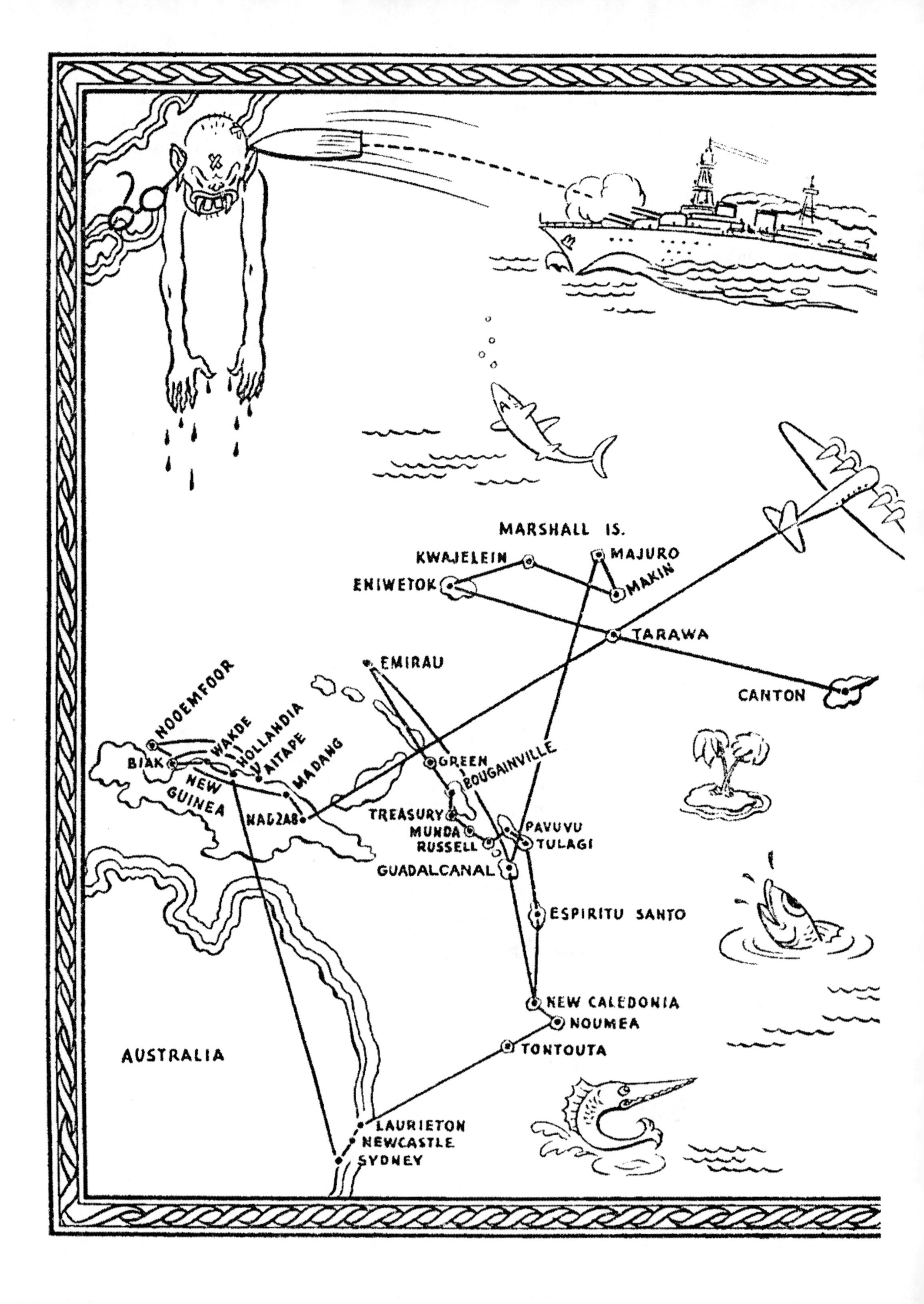

MARSHALL IS.
KWAJELEIN
MAJURO
ENIWETOK
MAKIN
TARAWA
EMIRAU
CANTON
NOOEMFOOR
WAKDE
HOLLANDIA
AITAPE
BIAK
NEW
GUINEA
MADANG
NADZAB
GREEN
BOUGAINVILLE
TREASURY
MUNDA
RUSSELL
PAVUVU
TULAGI
GUADALCANAL
ESPIRITU SANTO
NEW CALEDONIA
NOUMEA
TONTOUTA
AUSTRALIA
LAURIETON
NEWCASTLE
SYDNEY

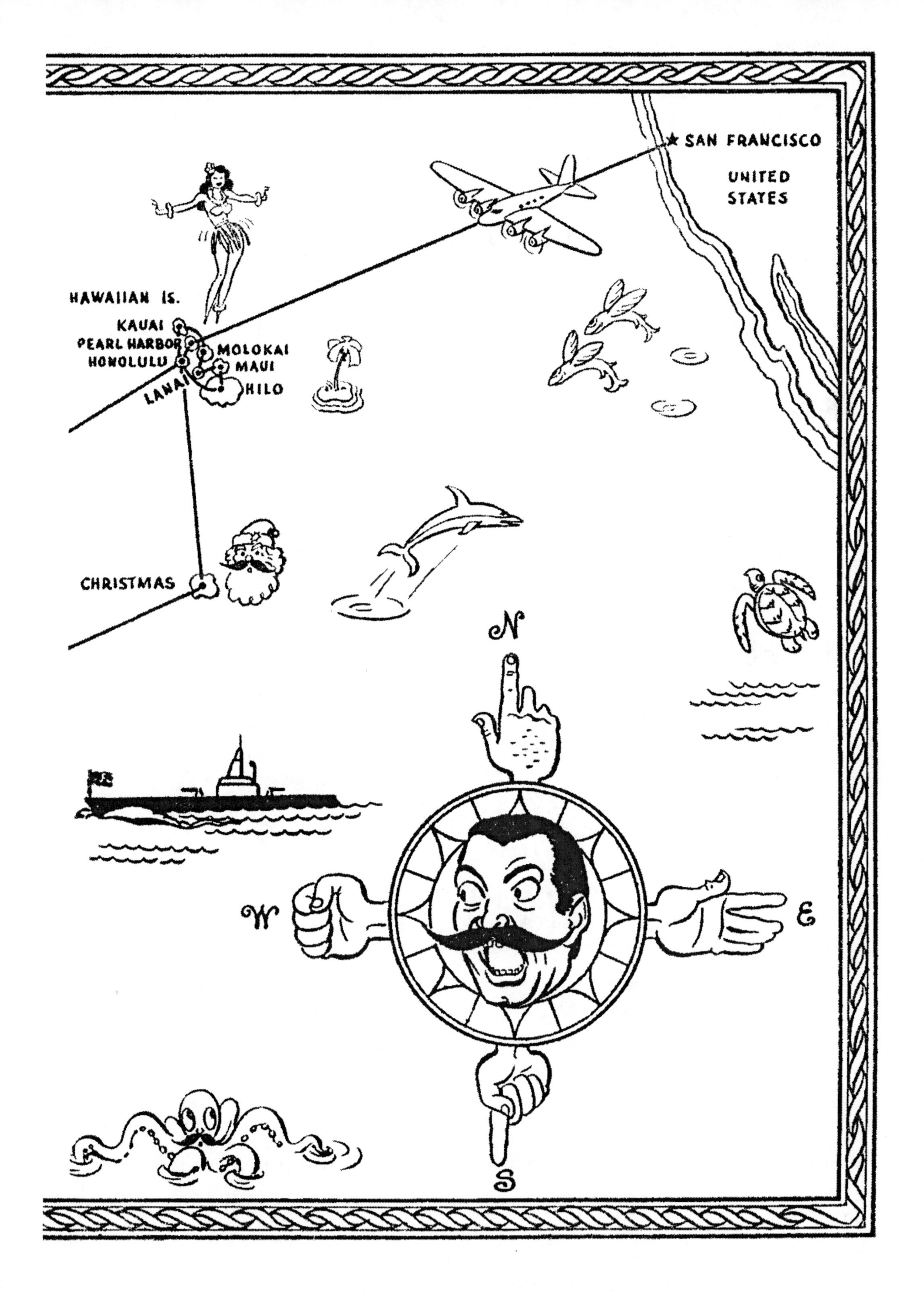
SAN FRANCISCO
UNITED
STATES
HAWAIIAN IS.
KAUAI
PEARL HARBOR
MOLOKAI
HONOLULU
MAUI
LANAI
HILO
CHRISTMAS
N
W
E
S

| U. S. O. UNIT | DATE | PLACE | AUDIENCE |
|---|---|---|---|
| *#130* | *July 29* | *Majuro* | *4,500* |

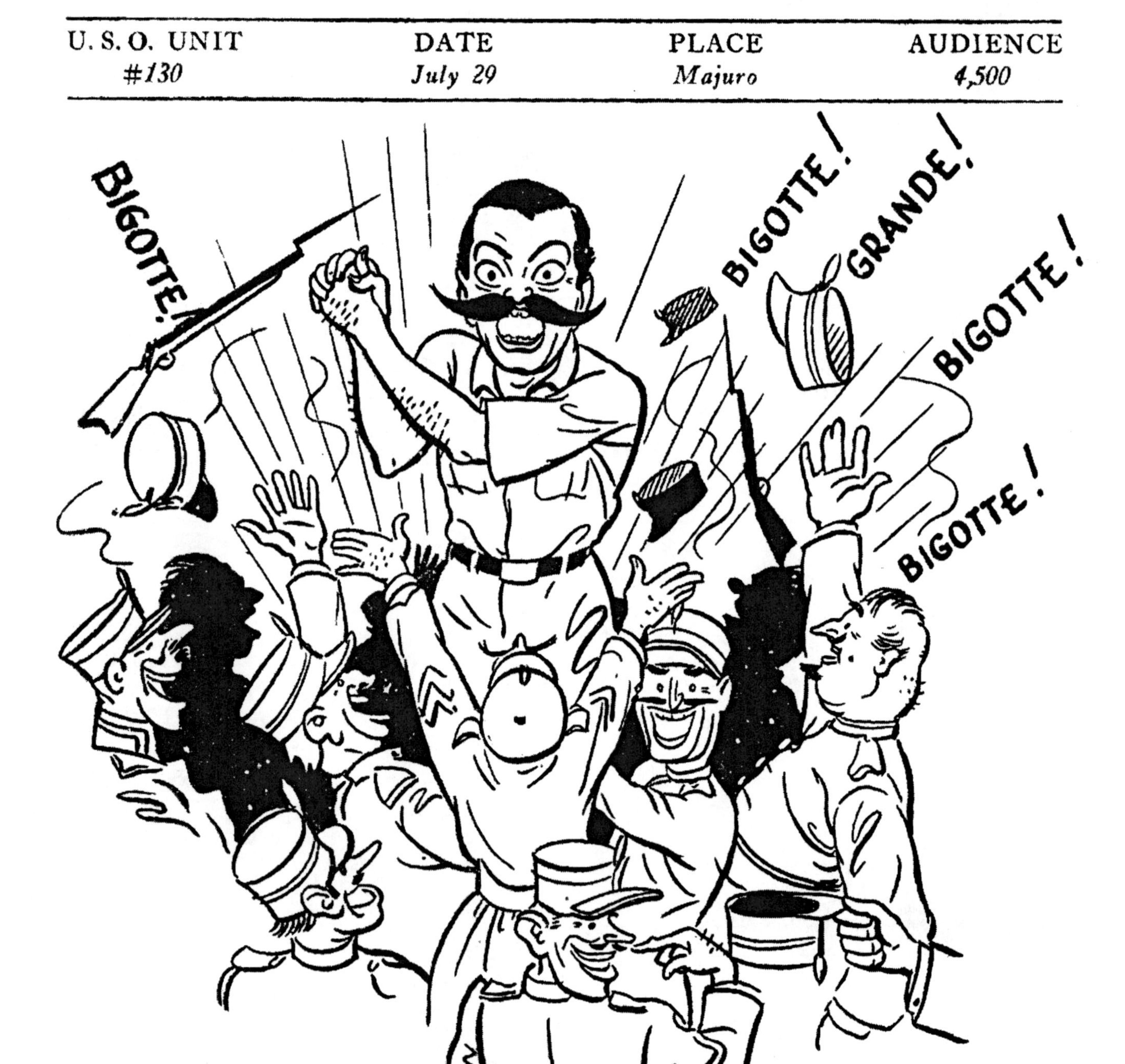


**WE GIVE A SHOW FOR THE NATIVES ON MAJURO**
**or**
**YOU SHOULD HAVE HEARD THE PINS DROP**

FLYING from Makin to Majuro that morning I felt in a meditative mood. What was it that had brought me all the way from a humble Boston schoolboy to this great job of traveling all over the world to entertain our fighting men? There were just two words that could answer it—*fight* and *work*. All my life I have fought work. It is surprising how often I have won.

All of a sudden both of my ears popped. It meant the "Seventh Heaven" was sitting down on the island of Majuro. How did I know this? Was it clairvoyance? Was it some jungle instinct I had developed? Or was it the pilot yelling, "We're sitting down on Majuro Island!"

He really knew how to fly that plane. They say a good pilot flies by the seat of his pants. He was so good he had worn out four pairs.

A native delegation met us at the plane. They were led by a very old white man. He seemed to be their king. Some of the men on the island said he was a descendant of Captain Christian of "Mutiny On The Bounty" fame. I couldn't believe this. He didn't resemble Clark Gable at all.

I wondered how it must feel to be a ruler. Then my thoughts soared higher. I wondered how it must feel to be a yard stick. I know that if I were in this man's place, if I were leader of a thousand ferocious natives, there is one thing I would certainly do. I would get out of there as soon as possible!

Hope took one look at the natives and said, "It looks like I'm on location for another one of my Road pictures!" Then he glanced at the old king and said, "My! hasn't Crosby aged!"

I tried to be friendly with the natives, but I just couldn't understand a word they were talking about. I didn't know enough about the Brooklyn Dodgers.

The ancient white man gave a signal to his followers and they began an island dance to the accompaniment of the tom-toms. I asked the old man where these strange primitive rhythms came from. He told me they came from a far away country, which, in their tongue, was called "The Palladium."

When the natives had finished putting on their show for us, we decided the least we could do was return the compliment. It seems I had swiped a compliment when they weren't looking. Although they hadn't asked us to, we went ahead and gave our show for them.

Hope started off with his usual monologue. For ten minutes he told jokes, and for ten minutes there was a deafening silence.

Bravely he continued.

Once he stopped cold. He thought he heard a chuckle from the back row. He listened. It was only a bull frog calling to his mate.

Again Hope turned to us and in a funereal voice muttered, "If this whole island were a frying pan, it wouldn't be big enough to hold the omelet I'm producing today."

A Naval officer explained to him that the natives didn't laugh because they didn't understand. Then Patty came out and did her dance. The natives smiled. They understood.

When Frances sang, the native faces broke into broad grins. Great, I thought. At last the show was going over. But then we discovered the true reason for their smiles. They thought we were auctioning off the girls.

One other time we had a similar experience with an audience that didn't understand. During our Caribbean trip, a group of Puerto Rican soldiers asked Hope to give a show for them. They couldn't understand a word of English and he couldn't understand a half a word of Spanish.

Hope's monologue proceeded in the following manner: Joke, no laugh; joke, no laugh; big joke, big no laugh! Hope was desperate. He wrung his hands, but still no laugh. The Puerto Ricans' faces looked like they were all in straight-jackets. Finally Hope signed off with, "Que Pasa?" which means in Spanish, "How goes it?" This brought down the house. The soldiers were so happy to learn that Bob Hope spoke Spanish.

I followed Hope on the stage and as I appeared, there was a tremendous ovation. I opened my mouth. They cheered for ten minutes. I closed my mouth. How could I top that? I was puzzled. Even that brought applause. They pointed at me, looked at each other, laughed and yelled, "Bigotte! Bigotte grande!" We were unable to go on with the show until we found out what I had done to inspire such a commotion. It turned out that I looked exactly like the Governor of the Island. He wore a big mustache (bigotte grande) which was the duplicate of mine.

Hope said, "from now on, Colonna, watch your step. I've finally found a guy who can replace you."

"Okeh," I said, "then *I* can be the governor of Puerto Rico!"

A shot rang out. The revolution had

started.

But getting back to Majuro (and I'm glad we are), we did three shows on the island, entertaining 4500 soldiers.

For relaxation we went swimming in the ocean. Here the water is very warm, and so clear you can see the bottom. I looked down and there I could see a little black crab nipping at my toes. Egad! what am I standing here for?

I'll tell you what I was standing there for. There was a beautiful Army nurse swimming five yards away. Hope tried to make an impression by swimming way out from the shore by himself, when suddenly he set up a terrific thrashing and splashing in the water. We sat around the beach watching him and wondering idly whether or not there would be any life insurance. At last we got our answer. A minute or two later he came walking up the sand dragging a dead octopus. The nurse wasn't the least bit impressed and walked away. Hope, dejected, unscrewed the cap and let the air out of the octopus.

All in all it was one of the pleasantest afternoons of our trip. Tony brought his guitar along. We were entertaining some Seabees when Frances and Patty appeared in their bathing suits. Two hours later Bob came by and dug our trampled bodies out of the sand. Hope told the girls to yell "Fore!" from now on before they walked by.

*Even the octopus hissed him.*

| U. S. O. UNIT | DATE | PLACE | AUDIENCE |
|---|---|---|---|
| *#130* | *July 30* | *Guadalcanal* | *1,500* |

**THE NATIVES ON GUADALCANAL**
**or**
**BEAUTY HINTS FROM THE SOUTH PACIFIC**

ON our way from Majuro to Guadalcanal we stopped off at Tarawa. We did a show for 1,500 men and took the rest of the day off. We needed it. So did the 1,500 men!

We spent most of the day caressing the bunks. Before I turned in, Hope gave me a rubdown. I looked at the bottle of liniment he was using. Something aroused my suspicions. Maybe it was the picture of a horse on the label.

"Hey, Hope!" I exclaimed, "what kind of liniment is this? It says, 'Good for man or beast.' "

"That's all right," Hope said, "use what you want. I'll give the rest to a man."

That Hope! Always joking. He rubbed the horse liniment into my tired carcass.

"How do you feel now?" Hope asked when he was finished.

I neighed contentedly.

Hope bent over me and tucked the covers around my neck. I thought this was very sweet of him until he stopped and said, "Tell me again. How do you tie a hangman's knot?"

I said nothing. I just looked up at him

with my big, brown eyes. This always scares him away.

I looked about the clean, quiet little room. Here was comfort!

I slept most of the day, until Hope came along, woke me up, and said we were going to see the picture of the battle of Tarawa that had been fought on this island a year before. The men had built themselves an open-air theater. It was a sort of Grauman's Chinese with the accent on Japanese.

These island theaters show all the latest pictures. Once during a Jap air raid, Errol Flynn jumped right out of the screen and shot down three Jap planes, directed by Mike Curtiz.

Next day we landed on Guadalcanal. Suddenly our pilot zoomed and circled. His first pass had showed him a lone Seabee with a bulldozer, just completing the last half of the landing field. By the time we had circled again, the field was completed. The reason it took so long was that the Seabee had taken time out to level the ball park.

It's amazing what our Seabees create and accomplish under the most miserable conditions. Talk about speed! We passed an area that was nothing but a foul, uninhabitable swamp. Two hours later we passed that same area again. I fell right in it.

Just to show you how fast these men work, the commanding officer was standing on a bare patch of ground and he said to one Seabee:

"I want you to build my headquarters here."

"Okay, sir," the Seabee said, "close the door as you go out."

The average Seabee thinks more of his bulldozer than he does of his right arm—except when he's out on dates.

Here we met Lieutenant Benn Reyes, combat photographer with the Fifth Air Force. Benn hails from our hometown, Hollywood. He got quite a kick out of showing us home folks the sights of Guadalcanal. We borrowed Benn's jeep and painted our own command letters on it.

Pacific commands were always identified by initial contractions. For example, the letters USAFISPA painted on a jeep meant that it belonged to the United States Armed Forces in the South Pacific Area. Also, COMAIRSOLS meant Commander for Air in the Solomons. Not to be outdone by this clever abbreviation, we devised our own command letters for the jeep. BOJERFRAPATOBAR stood for Bob-Jerry-Frances-Patty-Tony-Barney. If you think this was bad, you should see it upside down—

RABOTAPARFREJOB

That's just the way it looked the day our jeep hit the ditch.

We took the BOJERFRAPATOBAR to the local Mosquito Network Station. There we did a show for Captain Spencer Allen, former Chicago announcer. We were just in time to hear the "Atabrine Cocktail Hour." This is a program of recorded music played every afternoon to remind the men to take their Atabrine, a synthetic drug used to combat malaria.

The broadcast emanates from a fictitious night club called "The Lizard Lounge overlooking lovely Lunga Lagoon." It's sort of a Make-Believe Ballroom—selling make-believe quinine.

I decided to take a couple of these Atabrine pills. I figured that any program with as big a listening audience as this one had must have a good product. I gulped the pills down. Somebody had neglected to inform me that they turn your skin a golden yellow. I found out when I looked in the mirror. There I stood, a 14-karat Colonna!

After the broadcast, Hope said, "Come on, Golden Boy, we're going over to have a feast with Benn Reyes!"

Benn is a very fine cook. Spaghetti is his specialty. Ever so often his wife sent him all the needed condiments, and once he got these, he really went to town.

I ate more of that spaghetti than I have ever eaten in my life. Naturally, I had to show the gang how spaghetti should be eaten. I spun my fork around in it until I had a goodly portion at my command and then I drew it into my mouth with a great inhalation.

Once in trying to exhibit my genius, I

sucked in not only the spaghetti, but also everything on the table that wasn't nailed down. Benn spent twenty minutes trying to get the knives and forks out of my mouth.

Well nourished we left Benn's table and went to give a show at the Service Command Center.

The Service Center is run by the Red Cross, and along side it the G.I.'s have opened their own row of shops. These little shops were no more than a few up-ended boxes or old oil drums. But business was as flourishing as on the main street of a metropolis. One of the more exclusive shops was appropriately named "Gunny-Sack's Fifth Avenue." Here the G.I. pitchman would trade or sell anything from cat's eye jewelry to souvenirs made from Jap shells and wristwatch bands made of bits of metal from Jap planes. I tried to buy a wristwatch band for my wife, but the shop was out of stock. I asked him when he expected some more in.

He said, "Just as soon as the Japs come over again."

From these G.I. merchants the natives have learned a great deal about bargaining. In the early days of the American occupation the natives would work all day for a cigarette butt. Of course, this doesn't seem so strange when you remember that once Americans would stand in line all day and not even get a cigarette butt. Later on the natives found out there were big cigarette butts called cigarettes, and they demanded these as pay. That wasn't so bad, even when the day's wage rose to a package, but now if you want a native to tote a board across the street, he says "L.S.M.F.T." which is native for "Shoot the carton to me, Barton."

Although the natives got the better of the deal with the G.I.'s on the cigarettes, the G.I.'s won out with the atabrine pants. The natives go wild about brightly-colored clothes. For a brilliant piece of cloth they would trade their knives and jewelry. An enterprising G.I. discovered that his atabrine tablets dissolved in water made an excellent yellow dye. He began dyeing undershirts and pants bright yellow, and trading them to the natives. Before long the whole island looked like peeling day in a banana factory. The natives wore these shirts and pants in the customary manner—tied around their heads.

You can't blame the natives for going overboard on these colored clothes. They hadn't had any previous experience with Hart, Schaffner and Marx. Heretofore their bodies were bared to the elements save for a little breech-clout or "Lap-Lap." A "Lap-Lap" is merely a cloth that covers the lap, fore and aft.

By the time we arrived at the island, the natives had taken to wearing G.I. shoes and socks. They generally wore the socks over the shoes to preserve their polish. Best of all they like to wear raincoats. At the first sign of a cloud, their hearts beat wildly with excitement. The entire tribe don their raincoats and the chief beats on the rain drums. If the cloud turns out to be an impostor and passes over dry, the whole tribe beats on the chief.

On the other hand, if they are blessed with a downpour, they all run out, wrap their raincoats around them—and go scampering around barefoot in the rain—usually in mud up to their knees.

I thought of starting my own business on Guadalcanal, selling raincoats with built-in showers. Of course all transactions would be on credit: a pig down and four octopi a month. At eight legs per octopus, my business should have quite a turnover. I had even planned a name for my shop: "Colonna's Cloudburst Clothiery, We Guarantee You'll Get Soaked."

A cute little device the natives used to beautify themselves was to thrust bones through their noses. You could always tell a dreamer among them. He would have a wish-bone dangling from his nostrils. I was quite the gay blade around the tribe. They admired my mustache. Never before had they seen a bone through the nose with a fur coat on it.

They all had frizzy hair, originally black, but now tinted with various shades of red. It seems that they would apply a mixture of lime and water to it to keep insects away. The powerful lime solution bleached the hair red.

It also loosened the scalp a little for the convenience of head hunters.

It was quite a sight to see these natives in the audience at our shows. There they would sit with their red hair, bone through the nose, green raincoats, yellow trousers, and G.I. shoes. It looked like technicolor had run amuck.

These inhabitants of Guadalcanal were inveterate show-goers. They attended the nightly movies given for the troops as well as all the traveling U.S.O. shows. Their sense of humor was slightly different from ours and they'd always laugh at the wrong places.

Hope was pleased by this. He remarked, "This is the ideal audience. The soldiers laugh at the jokes and the natives fall out of their seats at the straight lines. It's egg-proof!"

| U. S. O. UNIT | DATE | PLACE | AUDIENCE |
|---|---|---|---|
| *#130* | *July 31* | *Emirau* | *14,000* |
| | *August 1* | *Green Island* | *15,000* |

**THERE'S NO PLACE LIKE EMIRAU**
**or**
**WHY NATIVES LEAVE HOME**

WE LEFT Guadalcanal in a P.B.Y. P.B. stands for patrol bomber and Y. stands for—I don't know why! It is an airplane with duck instincts. It can float or fly. This is a great convenience for the passengers. They have their choice of airsickness or seasickness.

As we took off from the bay, I once again proved what a thoughtful man I am. As always, I strapped on everybody's parachute. And, as always, everybody made me give theirs back to them.

Time flew; and so did we, but I'll bet Time

didn't get as bored as me! (Poem thrown in—no extra charge.) Perhaps it surprised you to hear that I am a poet. I'll have you know I once wrote for the *Saturday Evening Post*. And they sent it to me.

Before we could say "Emirau," we were there. In fact, we were still trying to say it long after we landed.

Hope looked down on this little bit of land called Emirau and exclaimed, "So that's what happened to that divot I dug last month at Lakeside!"

For those of you who are not familiar with golf, a divot is a piece of earth that flies through the air, down the fairway, straight for the hole, when all the time you wished it was the ball. Replacing the divot, I will tee off on the subject of golf.

The word "golf" springs from the Dutch "kolf," which, in turn, springs from laryngitis. Some people credit the original of the game to the Dutch, others to the Scots. It has always been Greek to me. According to the dictionary, and I quote, "The object of golf is to put the ball into each hole, using as few strokes as possible." How few golfers read the dictionary!

I have been working on my own game lately and I have managed to cut a few strokes off my score. I now shoot in the low thousands.

Hope played golf on every island where there was a golf course. The G.I.'s liked to watch him play. It seems that every time he teed off, they had another fox hole. He is really a very fine golfer. I will never forget the day he shot an eagle. I learned a lot that day. Primarily, that eagle meat is tough to eat.

The island commander, Brigadier General Joseph Boyd, showed us around the island and then took us to his quarters. On the way we met some G.I.'s who were reading the current issue of *Yank,* the Army's overseas magazine. It's sort of a cross between *Time* and *Esquire*. It has perhaps the greatest coverage of pin-up girls. Perhaps. Just a moment while I consult my files and verify this fact. (PAUSE: 1 minute.) Just as I thought—strike out the perhaps!

Due principally to *Yank,* our fighting men were the best informed in the world.

At Emirau we discovered that the latest issue of *Yank* was dedicated to our overseas troupe. Of course, I took this with a grain of salt, along with twelve copies of the magazine.

I sauntered up to one of the men reading the magazine, and in my own carefree way I pointed to my picture and exclaimed, "Well, well, what do we have here?"

In surprise they looked up at me, then back to my picture, then up at me again.

One of them said, "We've just spent half an hour looking at your pictures. Do you have to rub it in by showing up in person?"

I gave them my gay little laugh, kicked dirt in their faces, and moved on.

General Boyd had a nice house overlooking the water. He had converted the main room into a museum. It contained trophies and souvenirs which his men had picked up in their Pacific campaigns. The General asked Hope if he had found any curious objects during his trip that might be added to the museum collection. They had practically come to terms when I wrecked the deal. I refused to get up on the pedestal.

One of the General's prize souvenirs was a pair of high-powered binoculars captured from a Jap artillery outfit. They were placed on a stand where they commanded a view of the bay and the shipping. I was fascinated by these glasses. Through them I could see far out to sea. Suddenly, while I was peering, a fantastic monster arose out of the waves. It was oval shaped, dead white in color, with a circle of blue surrounding a central black spot. Altogether the most hor-

rible thing I have ever seen. I was about to collapse in terror when I discovered that the monster was only Hope's eyes. He was looking in the other end of the binoculars.

"Egad! Hope, I thought you were a squid."

"You should have known it was my eye!" Hope replied. "When have you ever seen a bloodshot squid?"

We told General Boyd our next stop was Green Island

He said, "I hope you'll like it. The rocks are white, the coral sand is pink, and the water is blue. That's why they call it Green Island."

The first impression I got when we arrived at Green Island was that it would be out of a job when the war was over. It is a tropical Paradise Lost, surrounded by water, which is the only reason the natives don't leave it.

The men entertained us with a wonderful exhibition of shooting. I was amazed at their ability. They shot the finest dice I'd ever witnessed.

About the only diversions on this island were shooting dice and reading a book. There were about 400 pairs of dice on the island and about 400 pages in the book. The title, incidentally, was "Seven Come Eleven."

For those of you who have never shot dice, what do you do with your money? You can buy a pair of dice for as low as fifteen cents. But in this game, it's not the initial investment, it's the upkeep. The way the game goes is like this. Suppose you're betting against a fellow who rolls a seven. And then he rolls another seven. And then he rolls another seven. And then—what are you standing around for? Go home. You're broke.

I once played in a game where a fellow rolled nine sevens in a row. Later they found lead in the dice. And later they found lead in him.

We were there to bring home to them. One fellow looked at me and said, "You didn't have to bring the dust mop."

The Seabees built a replica of the famous corner, Hollywood and Vine, for the arrival of the Hope troupe. It was a very faithful reproduction, complete with street light, fire plug, mail box, and patrolling M.P.'s. The scene looked so real to me as I stepped out of the jungle, that I headed right for the imitation Owl Drug store. I was promptly arrested for jay-walking.

Hope met with quite a nasty catastrophe. He tried to mail a letter in the pseudo mail box and the monkey who lived there bit him. He had mistaken Hope's hand for a special delivery bunch of bananas.

From Hollywood and Vine, Green Island Version, we went to the recreation center, which was also a base for P.T. boats. Here we did our show.

"That's a fine thing!" Hope said. "You really have to work to hold an audience that's sitting in P.T. boats with the motors running."

After the show I made a casual request for a drink of water. The way they acted you would think water was one of the most precious things on the island. It is.

There is no fresh water supply on Green. All their water is distilled from sea water by huge evaporators. This seemed quite a waste of money to me. A hundred thousand dollars worth of distillery and all that comes out is plain water.

While we were here, Patty had a birthday and all of us threw a party for her, complete with cake and candles. We all toasted her with our hundred proof $H_2O$, straight from the distillery. Patty was so thrilled by the party that she said she would like to give each of us a big hug and kiss. All at once our little troupe numbered 15,000 men. Those G.I.'s have good ears.

When we were ready to leave for Bougainville, the Green Island band came down to the air strip and serenaded us. They said they would have met us at our arrival, but the only song they knew was Aloha, which means farewell. I informed them that Aloha could also mean hello. The band-master turned to one of the players and said, "See, I told you that excuse wouldn't go over."

A-A-A-A-AH MEN!

| U. S. O. UNIT | DATE | PLACE | AUDIENCE |
|---|---|---|---|
| *#130* | *August 2* | *Bougainville* | *30,000* |
| | *August 3* | *Bougainville* | *25,000* |

## MESSAGE TO BOUGAINVILLE or "GUVMAN I SALIM DISPELA TOK"

OUR P.B.Y. set us down on Bougainville. During our stay here our mail caught up with us. It did my heart good to think that somebody in the states still thought of me, even if it was the Southern California Gas Company.

Just to show you how long it has been since we last received mail, Tony got two letters from his girl. In the first she asked him why he hadn't written to her. The second thanked him for his lovely letter.

While we were reading our mail, a soldier came up to me and said, "Shall I take your order, sir?" It was Al Sanchez. He knew me very well when he was a waiter at the Hollywood Brown Derby. In fact, he knew me so well, he always made me tip him *before* he served me.

"Al," I said, "this is a small world."

He said, "No, just a big Army."

Al had a curious document. It was a pamphlet the Australian Government had sent to the natives on neighboring Buka during the Jap occupation. He showed me the epistle and this is what it looked like:

**GUVMAN I SALIM TOK LONG OL BOI BUKA**

LONG YAR SIPO, JAPAN I KAM PAIT SITIL LONG YUMI NA OL I KISIM NUKINI NAP LONG LAE NA SALAMAUA.

PAS TAIM MIPELA I NO SITRON. NAU MIPELA SITRON PINIS NA AMERICA I KAM HALIPIM MIPELA. SOLDIA BILOG YUMI I RAUS IM PINIS OL JAPAN LONG LAE NA SALAMAUA NA KARIM PAIT LONG HAP BILOG MADANG. SOLDIA BILOG AMERICA I KOSUA PINIS LONG BIKBUKA, LONG PURUATA, NA WOKIM PLES BALUS LONG TOROKINA. BALUS BILOG YUMI NAU LUKAUTIM SIP NA LAÑIS BILOG JAPAN BILOG DAUNIM, NA LIKLIK TAIM JAPAN I ANGRI, I NOGAT KAIKAI.

KAIKAI BILOG YUPELA DASOL. YUPELA KILIA LONG JAPAN NA KOHAIT GUT LONG WOK LONG BUS. YUPELA WONTAIM MERI NA PIKININI NA PIK, OL I KOHAIT GUT LONG BUS NA WEITIM MIPELA.

KIAP BILOG YUPELA I STAP WONTAIM SOLDIA BILOG YUMI. YUPELA NOKAN PRET. GUVMAN I SAVI JAPAN I PULIM PLANTI BOI BILOG HALIPIM OL. MASKI, YUPELA NOGAT TOROVEL LONG DISPELA PASIN, TOROVEL LONG JAPAN DASOL. GUVMAN I SORI TUMAS LONG YUPELA, OLTAIM TING LONG YUPELA. YUPELA KOHAIT GUT NA WEITIM TOK BILOG GUVMAN.

**GUVMAN I SALIM DISPELA TOK.**

Inspiring, isn't it? Al told me that the message was written in pidgin English. The spelling in pidgin English is pretty horrible, but, after all, what can you expect from a pigeon? (They can't even spell pidgin right.)

I will now reward your patience with a translation. Follow closely. It goes like this:

**GOVERNMENT HE SENDEM TALK (MESSAGE) ALONG (TO) ALL BOYS ON BUKA**

Long years before, Japan he come fight with you-me (us), na (and) he bring war to Lae and Salamaua.

Past time (then) me fellow I no strong.

Now me strong finish (very strong) and America he come helpum me. Soldiers belong you-me (our soldiers) he raus (German for scram) him finish all Japs at Lae and Salamaua and carry the fight up to Madang. Soldier belong America he go a-shore at Big Buka (Bougainville) and Puruata, and workum a place for airplanes at Torokina. Airplanes belong us now lookoutum for ships and lands belong Japs and down 'em, and in a little time Japan he get angry he no got food.

All the food belongs to you fellows, that's all! You get clear of Japs and ko hait (go hide) in gut (jungle) long walk long bus (in other words, get a helluva ways into the jungle). You fellows want your Mary (women) and pickaninnies (children) and pigs (pigs), all go hide in jungle and waitum me fellow.

Kiap (Chief, meaning government representative) belong you fellows he is staying with our soldiers. You no can fret (don't worry). Government knows that Japs pullem plenty of you boys to help them. By'm'by, you got no trouble along this line, trouble will be Japan's, that's all! Government he sorry too much (very sorry) for you and all time think about you. You go hide in jungle and wait for message from your government.

**GOVERNMENT HE SENDEM THIS FELLOW TALK**

"Doesn't it sound convincing?" Al said.

I replied: "You fella no bother me fella. I ko hait in jungle."

With this I was off in the manner of the best Buka boy.

Bougainville is known for its dense jungles. This must be where Tarzan goes when he dies. Along the way I saw the native flora and fauna. Two of the nicest girls I ever met!

From out of nowhere came a native medicine man, a terrifying specimen of humanity. His face was painted in green and orange stripes, and he was wearing a black silk top hat and polka dot sandals. Without knowing what I was doing, I burst into hysterical laughter right in his face.

I said, "Ubangi?"

And he did. Right in my kisser!

I ran away from him in a frenzy. I'm only sorry I wasn't in a Jeep. After I had run until I was exhausted, I heard a cry coming from the distant swamp. The voice moaned plaintively, "Chloeeee! Chloeeeee! Chloeeeeeeeee!

I called, "Why do you keep yelling 'Chloeeee'?"

The voice answered, "Can't remember the second line!"

It was Hope. Once again he had come to my rescue!

Bob led me back to civilization, and civilization demanded that he lead me back to the jungle. But Bob was too tired to make the trip again.

During our stay on Bougainville we were the guests of General O. W. Griswold. His famous Fourteenth Corps had won this island in record time and later they went on to the Philippines, where their fighting record became part of American military history.

General Griswold had made our stay so pleasant that I told him I felt I could stay here forever. But that night before going to bed I asked where the distant artillery fire was coming from. The General told me there was still a fair-sized Jap force being held in check in the hills only a short jeep-ride away.

"What are we waiting for?" I answered. "Let's get out of here!"

Tony complained of the noise made by the big guns. He yelled, "It's disturbing my sleep!"

Barney whispered, "Shut up! Do you want the Japs to overhear you and get mad at the whole troupe?"

But we forgot about the Japs in the hills (that's a lie if I ever heard one) and the next morning got down to the business of entertaining the G.I.'s.

After the show the men showed their appreciation by presenting Frances and Patty with bouquets made up of exotic orchids, gardenias, gorgeous flame flowers, and camellias. These flowers grow wild on Bougainville. I could have made a fortune selling dandelions here. In the United States orchids are quite expensive. Some people pay as much as $10 for a single orchid. Why pay $10 for an orchid when you can pick all the orchids you want on Bougainville, and it won't cost you a cent.

Let's figure it out. Plane fare to this island is around $440 one way. You will need refrigeration equipment, which would come to around $350, and—er—well! $10 is pretty cheap for an orchid.

Beautiful flowers aren't the only things the people of Bougainville have to boast about. The largest centipedes in the world are found here. They don't make very good house pets because of an objectionable trait they possess. Their poison can kill a man. In fact, it's not too healthy for the women-folk.

These centipedes have a nasty habit of crawling into a man's bed at night or invading his clothes after he has taken them off. This should explain why I spent the night fully dressed, hanging from a clothes-line. Hope said he couldn't see why I didn't go back to bed, as he carefully clothespinned his ears to the rope.

During our stay on Bougainville, fate double-crossed me. I was in need of a hair-cut. I passed a tree painted red, white and blue, and, sure enough, behind it was a little thatched hut which was marked "Barber Shop." Strolling in not unlike a man approaching a high tension wire, I seated myself in the barber's chair, which for local color was designed to resemble a log from a palm tree.

The G.I. barber must have noticed the expression of fear on my face because he steadied me by remarking, "You don't have to worry about me. I'm a first-class tonsorial artist. Had quite a business in Glendale."

With this he took out a pair of scissors that looked like they had spent the greater part of their life clipping wire. I felt like asking him to give me chloroform. Before I could get my mouth open, I heard a snap of the clippers and a tuft of my locks fell to the floor. I believe I detected part of my ear among the rubble.

Ten minutes later the barber said he was through with me. The feeling was mutual. For weeks afterwards I went around looking like a French Poodle that somebody had sabotaged.

Bob and I discovered that our friendship had been cemented more than ever on this island. This was due to the type of showers they had in the Solomons. A man without a friend never took a shower. Our bathing routine went something like this: Bob stood on a platform and I climbed a ladder holding a five-gallon can of water in my hands. After he had lathered himself sufficiently, I nonchalantly poured the five gallons of water down on him until his bath was completed. Then we changed places. Once our friendship nearly came to an end. While he was dropping the water on me, he forgot to hold on to the five-gallon can. I showed up at lunch with a five-gallon bump on my head.

Later that day we visited one of the smallest radio stations in the world. It was located in a foxhole and belonged to a fighter squadron. This station fed its daily programs to the camp by means of five speakers. The programs consisted of news broadcasts, request record programs, and live shows put on by local talent. Any of the men who had some jokes to tell and who wasn't needed for sentry duty could go on the air. A foxhole is a dangerous place to entertain. If your audience doesn't like your act, all they have to do is shovel dirt over you and your career is finished.

After we brushed ourselves off, we were told by a passing G.I. the local police wanted us. I won't say we were in a hurry to quit the vicinity, but the G.I. had to finish his sentence by radio: it seems the local police wanted us to watch them drill. We came out of the jungle and walked down to the village police station. This was a long native building with two green melons hanging out in front.

When we arrived, the chief of police asked us to review the parade of his men. The Bougainville Dick Tracys were smartly attired in "lap-laps." They marched up and down in front of our party, rifles slung over their shoulders. Then, as a complete switch, they disappeared into their grass huts. Just when we had decided the show was over, out they scampered again. This time they were carrying spears, poison-tipped arrows, bows and blow guns. We decided to make a run for it, but it was too late. The "law" had encircled us. As they leaped around us, shouting and brandishing their spears, I knew how Captain John Smith felt. I looked around for help, but all I saw was Hope, and he is certainly no Pocahontas!

When I felt one of the poison arrows tickling my chin, I jumped into Hope's arms. He was already in the arms of Barney Dean.

With an atom-splitting scream, the native police fell to their knees and thrust their spears and arrows into the ground, making a solid ring around us.

All of us fell to our knees, begging for mercy with one exception. I alone was

unmoved. I was dangling by the seat of my pants from a spear.

The escorting Australian officer assured us that the natives were not angry at us. I told him this couldn't be love. He explained they were merely trying to get over the idea that they were grateful to the white man for getting rid of the Japs. That was their way of saying "Thanks." I told him they'd better not leave any spears lying around, because they might not like the way I'd say "You're welcome."

"You mustn't feel that way," the officer said. "The significance of the wall of spears stuck into the ground is that the natives will protect you till the death."

"That's all very well," I replied, "but if they keep throwing spears around like that, 'the death' may come sooner than we want it to."

With that the dance of the constabulary was over and they reclaimed their spears. It left me with a great respect for law and order on Bougainville. If that's the way they thank you, you can imagine what you'd get for parking overtime in a restricted zone.

| U. S. O. UNIT | DATE | PLACE | AUDIENCE |
|---|---|---|---|
| *#130* | *August 4* | *Treasury Island* | *20,000* |

### TREASURY ISLAND
### or
### YO HO HO AND A BOTTLE OF POP!

WE had been traveling by plane so much none of us knew whether we were on the ground or in the air. This is an important thing to know, especially if you're in the habit of going outside and taking a walk around the block. The block might be 30,000 feet below the front door. It was just like being on a merry-go-round with wings. We'd take off, land, do half a dozen shows, take off, land, do more shows, and take off again. I got so mixed up, I wore my parachute to bed no matter where I was. One night I had a nasty accident. I bailed out of a nightmare at three feet and nearly broke my neck. It seems I became panicky and pulled the wrong cord. I woke up on the floor without the pants to my pajamas.

Just as we landed on Treasury Island a flight of B-25's was coming in from a strike at Rabaul. We went over to greet the fellows as they climbed out of their planes. These men had just completed an extremely hazardous mission, and we weren't surprised to hear one of the flyers exclaim, "Boy, are we lucky!" But we nearly fell down when he added, "We're just in time to see the Bob Hope show."

Not even Hope could top that. What those men wanted was entertainment. We gave it to them.

After the show, we asked some of the men why this island was named Treasury. From where I was standing it looked like someone had run off with the treasury.

They told us that many of the natives claim it was the original Treasure Island celebrated by Robert Louis Stevenson in his famous book.

After looking around the island, I came to the conclusion that Bob Stevenson had a terrific imagination. I spent many hours digging for buried pirate gold. Did I get doubloons? Did I get pieces-of-eight? Did I get gold ingots? No, I got lumbago!

I turned a sad eye on my parrot perched on a piece of wreckage nearby. In cold tones he reproached me, "No more pieces-of-eight . . . mate! . . . Too late!"

But be that as it may, there really was a person, Long John Silver, I know, because he was a shipmate of my great, great grandfather, Short Change Colonna. Ah! Yes! There was a buccaneer without a buck to his name.

Short Change left many interesting documents for posterity. Searching through his papers, this is what I learned:

At one time there was a whole island in the Pacific populated by nothing but Colonnas. As far as the eye could see, nothing but Colonnas. They arrived for centuries in this remote part of the world, but eventually civilization came along and ruined them. A telephone system was installed on Colonna Island. It was called the Colonna Tel. and Tel. They were great gossips! One Colonna was appointed to print the phone book. As the days went by, the sheer monotony of printing the name Colonna over and over again drove him crazy. To stave off insanity, he tried spelling the names differently. Kolonna, Calynna, Quolonna, Cologna, even Bologna. This did not turn the trick. He went berserk and wiped out every Colonna on the island, including himself. Now, nothing but the moustaches of my ancestors Colonna remain there, but they are in good health and multiply rapidly. These moustaches have overcrowded the island, and every year thousands of them drift out to sea. Of course, this is what keeps the ocean well stocked with seaweed.

I related the history of my ancestry to Hope. He appeared puzzled. He knitted his brows, dropping one and purling the other.

"Colonna," Hope said, "I don't believe a word of what you're saying."

"Which word don't you believe?"

Bob was cross. "Colonna, where were you

when they passed out the brains?"

I smiled. "You ought to know. You were standing right behind me."

Bob looked at me and grinned. Good-natured Hope! He was always willing to take a rib. That's why I wear a steel vest.

But I seem to wander. Well, what do you expect in a travel book?

Between shows here we had the rare treat of riding in the cockpits of P-38's. The P-38 is a single-seat fighter, and the only way the cockpit can accommodate an extra person is when the radio is removed. I wedged myself in the place where the radio used to be and knelt hunched over the pilot, practically sitting on his shoulder. Once he forgot the radio was gone and started twisting my nose, trying to tune in on Saipan. That was silly. My antennae had picked up Guadalcanal. Suddenly we hit an air pocket. Now I know how a radio feels when a tube blows.

The way those fellows handle a plane makes you think they were born part bird. And the way I act in it makes you think I was born part coward. After a little banking and climbing, the pilot asked me how I'd like to go into a dive. I told him that would be wonderful, I could use a drink about now.

Before I knew it, he was taking me through an Immelmann. This maneuver is similar to riding a roller-coaster without benefit of tracks. The plane went into a deep dive, and just when it looked like the ground was going to smack me between the eyes, we shot up toward the sky. The pressure of coming out of that dive pulled my face out of alignment so much that my Adam's apple had ears. Just when I was convinced that all was lost, we snapped over on our backs and all *was* lost! Never in my life have I hated the Wright Brothers like I hated them then. Why couldn't they have been content to ride around New Jersey on their scooter bikes?

The monster in front of me spoke, "How'd you like that? I just came out of a snap-roll."

I sneered at him. "What's so great about that? I just came out of a coma!"

After the plane had landed, Hope came rushing up to me.

"Colonna, did the ride make you nervous?"

I was indignant. "Of course not!"

Hope tugged at my arm. "Then stop gnawing the wing off that plane."

When they came to tell me it was time to take off for Munda, I wrapped my arms around a tree and screamed hysterically, "I won't go! You can't drag me away from this tree!"

If you think I am exaggerating, the next time you're in Munda you'll see that very tree.

| U. S. O. UNIT | DATE | PLACE | AUDIENCE |
|---|---|---|---|
| *#130* | *August 5* | *Munda* | *15,000* |

## WE ENTERTAIN AT ANOTHER ISLAND or SUNDA, MUNDA, AND ALWA

WE got the same enthusiastic reception at Munda as elsewhere. The G.I.'s swarmed around me and asked, "Is that a real moustache?"

"No, it's a fake," I said, pulling another moustache out of my pocket. "This is the real one."

During the day we were the guests of the 93rd Infantry Division. Their commanding officer gave a buffet luncheon in our honor. They printed a special menu for the occasion. Hope got top billing on the menu, then Frances, Patty, Tony, and Barney. Here I found out just what the 93rd Infantry thought of me. My name came between the fresh shrimp and the stuffed olives. Of course I had one consolation. I could have been listed among the cheeses.

The Maitre d' Officers' Mess was T/Sgt. Roosevelt Parlor, a tall, good-looking, jovial negro. He used to be a railroad dining car chef. I told him he had a most unusual name. He replied with a broad grin, "I'm very proud of my name. You know, most of the Pullmans are named after me. You've heard of Parlor Cars, of course."

"Yes," I said, "and now that I think of it, a couple of Presidents were named after you too."

At all of the four shows we did on the island, I devoted my act to telling 15,000 men about my exploits as a hot pilot on Treasury Island. Did you ever hear 15,000 horse laughs? In spite of the jeering, I went on and told them I no longer feared the sky. I finally convinced all of them. All except one—myself.

There were a number of natives in the audience. We've seen more savages on this tour than you can shake a stick at. And if you've ever seen any of these natives, you'll understand why we didn't shake any sticks.

Frances had pictures taken with the native chief. He was a tall, powerful looking man. Muscles from head to toe. He even had muscles in his muscles. He shook hands with me so hard my eye teeth changed places. I now know what they mean by butter fingers. He really churned mine.

The chief insisted I have some betel nut. The natives all chewed it. It had a sort of a kick to it. It's like chewing 100 proof bubble gum. The betel nut stains your teeth black. As a result, whenever you part your lips it looks like the curtain rising on a minstrel show.

I wanted to show the chief I appreciated his hospitality, so in my best pidgin English I said, "Me fella likum betel nut, much much. That's all."

The chief shook his head at me and in his best plain old English said, "Civilization hasn't gone very far, has it?"

Ignoring his comment, I announced my decision.

"Big chief," I said, "me fella ko hait in jungle!"

He said, "Have you been reading that pamphlet too?"

But I was gone. Again I pushed my way into the jungle. This time my objective was a rare butterfly for my collection. Some men collect bear skins, some collect lion heads, others collect leopard pelts. But *they're* brave.

With my butterfly net cocked at a rakish angle, I penetrated deep into the thicket. And I must say, a couple of times the thicket penetrated deep into me. All at once I came upon a rare specimen of horrorculis monstroso-puss. To you, a Boris-Karloff-faced butterfly. I couldn't begin to tell you how valuable this insect is. I don't know myself. Fearlessly, I moved toward him and quick as a wink I swung my net!

But that butterfly outsmarted me. He dodged and flew right into my hair. He was seeking aid from the butterflies in my head.

Quick as a flash (I had to use a flash, I had no more winks left), I flushed him out of my hair. I grabbed him in my hand, but something told me to let him go. Did you know butterflies could bite? It seems this one had wasp blood in him — and Colonna blood in him too.

The next thing I remember the native chief was shaking me.

"You certainly let your imagination run away with you, Professor. You've been screaming about butterflies for twenty minutes. I've never seen betel nut affect a man that way before."

Embarrassed, I bowed low to the chief and scurried off. I had concealed a couple of betel nuts in my pocket. I was determined to go after that butterfly again in the privacy of my own room.

When I returned to the base, I found Bob taking treatments for a mild case of fungus on his feet (which the G.I.'s affectionately call "Jungle Rot"). This he had contracted at Guadalcanal.

Jungle Rot is not as serious as it sounds. It is like Athlete's Foot, Olympic Games variety. It made Hope's feet resemble a relief map of the New Hebrides.

At each base we visited, Bob received treatment, and each time he always had a clever remark ready for the doctor, such as "Ouch!", "Take it easy!", or "#$?*%&!". The last is a Russell Island word meaning "Lovely iodine you have here!"

Our P.B.Y. flew us all around the Russells. We got quite a laugh wherever we landed. Bob had painted a set of teeth on the nose of the ship. Under it he had written in big letters "P.B.Y." He told all the fellows it stood for "Pepsodent Brightens Yours."

The G.I.'s showed Bob and me how to take a bath out of a helmet. It's very simple. You fill the helmet with water, put in a cake of soap, and make thick, creamy suds. Then you put the helmet on your head, go about your business, and in the course of the next half hour you are thoroughly washed.

We used our new mess kits for mirrors. Bob was surprised at the way his features were distorted. Personally, I rather liked the way the mess kit reflected my face. I thought the fried egg on my forehead gave me quite a devil-may-care expression.

Having completed our beauty treatments, we were ready to visit other islands in the Russells group. We traveled around with the Navy in P.T. boats. P.T. stands for Patrol Torpedo, and that's about *all* it stands for. Anything else it will sink.

We had a date to entertain the First Marine Division on nearby Puvuvu. We took off in a number of Cub planes, used by the Army for spotting artillery. This was all right with me as long as the artillery didn't spot us. Each plane was a two seater carrying one of us and the pilot. After riding in a P.B.Y., a Cub seemed very slow. It sort of hangs up there in the sky, and rocks in the slipstream made by the seagulls whizzing past. It gives you the feeling that you're riding a kite with no strings attached.

From the air Puvuvu looks just like it sounds, with the accent on the PU. Waiting for us on the beach were 18,000 Marines. Veterans of Guadalcanal, Munda and Bougainville, they were preparing to go on to Iwo Jima, Okinawa, and glory.

These men had gathered from L.S.T.'s, L.C.I.'s, and many other landing craft which had been drawn up on the beach. The rigging and every vantage point on the ships were filled with thousands of men.

We circled low and buzzed them a couple of times, and then, since there was no airstrip on the island, the planes set down on a bumpy dirt road behind the stage.

The pilot I was riding with yelled, "Okay, Professor, pile out!"

As I picked myself out of the ditch, I called, "Pile out yourself. I've been out since the first bump!"

I wasn't the only one roughed up by the landing. Hope stood up next to me in the ditch and said, "Fancy meeting you here! You'd think Puvuvu airport could afford a better waiting room than this!"

The show we gave for the First Marine Division there on the beach probably won't be remembered long, but the show they went on to do for us will always be remembered.

| U. S. O. UNIT | DATE | PLACE | AUDIENCE |
|---|---|---|---|
| *#130* | *August 7* | *Guadalcanal* | *48,000* |
| | *August 8* | *Guadalcanal* | *38,000* |
| | *August 9* | *Tulagi* | *10,700* |
| | *August 10* | *Espiritu Santo* | *21,000* |
| | *August 11* | *Espiritu Santo* | *18,000* |
| | *August 12* | *New Caledonia* | *15,000* |
| | *August 13* | *New Caledonia* | *45,000* |

**GUADALCANAL, TULAGI, ESPIRITU SANTO AND NOUMEA**
**or**
**SHOOT THE BENZEDRINE TO ME, MARINE**

THE moment we arrived back at Guadalcanal, we were told that an aircraft carrier had arrived in the harbor. We beat it down to the pier and went out to the carrier. We did our show from the ship's plane elevator. This was a new experience. At one moment you would be looking into the smiling faces of a group of sailors, then would come a lifting sensation and you would find yourself eye to eye with a seagull.

Hope thought this was a very novel idea to perform on an elevator.

He said, "You don't have to worry about whether these fellows like you or not. If they don't care for your act, they don't have to say a thing. They just press a button and, Boom! You're walking the plank."

I thought that was a crazy remark for Hope to make. I laughed heartily. When I stopped laughing, I was soaking wet. And I didn't even hear the Boom! I will always regret that the only one who heard my last chorus of "Conchita" was a sturgeon. He appreciated it so much, he slipped me a fin.

But don't get me wrong. I love the little denizens of the deep. I am a great student of Izaak Walton. Many's the time I have gone to a mountain stream, flipped my rod, listened to the line sing out, and then started reeling. Heavy exercise always knocked me out.

There's nothing so delicious as a freshly hooked trout fried over an open fire, saturated in oil, with the vital juices lending a tang to the sauce, and those great big, red eyes looking up at you. Pardon me, I think I'm going to be sick!

On Tulagi we discovered another interesting fact about fish. So many ships had been sunk in the so-called Iron Bottom Bay that the sailors claimed the waters ran pure red with rust. I investigated the matter and found that the Navy men were understating the case. Not only was the water rusty, but all the fish were growing armor plate instead of scales. When you go fishing in Iron Bottom Bay you don't use worms, you bait your

hook with a magnet. If I thought you would swallow this line, I would go on to tell you that one of the sharks I caught is now being used for a radiator in my home.

We gave a show for the Navy at Tulagi.

Behind the stage there were rows of large quonset huts. I asked Lt. Reyes, who was still guiding our troupe, if these were to be our living quarters for the night.

He said, "You wouldn't be comfortable there. These huts are crammed with thousands of cases of beer."

I stared at him, eyes akimbo. "Well, we're used to putting up with hardships."

We had lunch aboard the repair ship, Dixie. Since we had had no breakfast, we were greatly in need of repair. As our P.T. boat drew up alongside, the ship's band broke into "Thanks For The Memory."

Hope stood at attention. He said, "Ah! that Pepsodent National Anthem!"

We were piped aboard by the boatswain's whistle. Then he piped Frances and Patty, and you should have heard him whistle!

For lunch we had what is generally known in the Solomons as Millionaire's Salad. It is a rare treat because it is made from the hearts of palm trees. Each tree contains only one heart and the tree must be cut down to secure it. I was about to help myself to a second portion when a spoon cracked down on my hand and Hope crooned in my ear, "That heart belongs to Patty."

After a sleepless night during which I dreamt about palm trees dancing around me and singing "Yours Is My Heart Alone," we moved on to Espiritu Santo in the New Hebrides. This island was commonly referred to as "Buttons," which was its code name. I suggested that as long as they were changing the name, they might as well make it more modern and call it Zipper. I put my suggestion through official channels and received a quick reply, to wit:

Mr. Jerry Colonna
U. S. O. Unit #130
Somewhere In The
South Pacific

re: Changing code name of Espiritu Santo from "Buttons" to "Zipper"

File No.: 34A-76983-buttons/zipper

Dear Sir:

a) Memorandum recommending change of code name of Espiritu Santo Island from "Buttons" to "Zipper" received 6 August by Bureau of Naval Terminology.

b) Referred to Bureau of Naval Intelligence. No intelligence found in suggestion.

c) Referred to Bureau of Naval Supply, attention Custodian of Wastepaper Depositaries.

d) Duly filed.

e) Action taken: As of this day the code name of Espiritu Santo remains "Buttons." "Zippers" are out for the duration.

(Signed) MAX SMETANA
Commander, U. S. N.
(Ex-tailor and button manufacturer)

I was quite downcast by this reaction to my suggestion until I discovered an identical letter on the back of the sheet. Then I knew Hope had typed it. Carbons always throw him.

A large American troopship, formerly a swank luxury liner, had been wrecked on the coast nearby. After the official salvage crews had taken off everything they wanted, the local G.I.'s did a little salvaging on their own hook. They scrounged everything they could get their hands on. Scrounge is a G.I. term meaning "if you can't lift it, get your buddy to help you."

As a result it was not unusual to walk into a small tent and find it furnished with a Louis Quinze bed, a Chippendale chair, or a Duncan Phyfe table. The sailors even went so far as to touch up some of the reproductions of famous paintings they had removed from the liner's salon. I peered into one of the tents and saw that Gainsborough's Blue Boy had worked himself up to Seaman 1st Class.

That night we went out to visit several of these ships and we got quite a kick out of the novel method they have of seeing movies. They tie up four or five submarines or destroyers side by side and put a screen up on the middle ship. Then the audiences crowd around the other ships and in this way all five are able to see the same movie. There is one drawback to this arrangement. If the commanding officer of one of the subs doesn't care for the picture, his section of the audience gets quite a ducking.

Hope remarked that he'd hate to appear in a picture shown under these conditions. "How could I concentrate on kissing Paulette Goddard with all those guns leveled at me?"

Several of the sailors who overheard this remark offered to change places with him.

From Buttons we flew to New Caledonia. We landed late at night on Tontouta air field. From there we took small planes, C-45's, forty miles to Noumea. You might ask why we didn't drive the forty miles. It's pretty hard driving in that kind of country at night. In fact, it's pretty hard driving in the middle of the day. No roads.

In Noumea we were put up at the Navy's Welfare Home. We were a little hurt at this. Imagine! We hadn't even done our show yet, and they thought we were ready for the Welfare Home.

Since we left Honolulu we hadn't been in such a large town. It was the first time Frances and Patty had seen another white woman in weeks. The rest of us were interested too.

The center of social life for the Allied officers was the Hotel Pacifique. I had just about finished correcting the spelling on the sign when somebody told me this was a French island. I passed this information on to Tony and he said:

"Now I understand what that girl meant by 'Non! non! non! non!' "

We strolled along the streets exchanging vive's with the French citizens. I was amazed to hear small children of four and five speaking better French than I could in high school. Some of them spoke better English too.

The Hotel Pacifique had been opened as a bar and club and had grown to be practically a million dollar enterprise. We visited it, and what entertainment! As the French say, Oo la la! cherchez la femme! This means, the food was great. That of course is a rough translation and not altogether true.

The enlisted men had the Triangle Club, an outdoor beer garden and sports arena where boxing tournaments were held. I went in and ordered a glass of beer. One sip sent me reeling. Then I realized that it wasn't the potency of the beer, but the fact that I was sitting too close to the ringside. Those boxers didn't care what they hit.

I got into a conversation with a Marine at my table. He told me a very interesting fact. It seems that New Caledonia is one of the few places in the world that produces nickel.

I pondered for a moment and then said, "Oh, you mean this place is sort of a slot machine with trees!"

He didn't think it was funny.

So I left. When I arrived back at the Welfare Home, I repeated the joke to Hope. He reacted quicker than the Marine. When I came to, I found the gang packing for Australia.

| U. S. O. UNIT | DATE | PLACE | AUDIENCE |
|---|---|---|---|
| *#130* | *August 14* | *Laurieton* | *64* |

**FORCED LANDING AT LAURIETON**
**or**
**OUR P.B.Y. GOES TO P.O.T.!**

OUR P.B.Y. headed for Sydney, Australia. The prospect of being in civilization once again thrilled me. I thought of a warm bath, a soft bed, plenty of fresh food, all of them waiting for me in Sydney.

Frances said, "Oh, won't it be wonderful to be in a place where there's a beauty parlor!"

The thought of it intrigued me! I've always had a weakness for manicurists.

Hope sat back in his seat and mused blissfully, "Aw, civilization! Cigarette lines, ration books, meatless Tuesdays, no vacancy, withholding taxes . . ."

With one accord we all yelled to the pilot, "Turn around! Back to Bougainville!"

On we flew down the Australian coast. The engines were purring smoothly. Most of the troupe were purring in their bunks, fast asleep. Hope was up front with the pilots, and I was reading. It was the most interesting book I had ever read. I hated to see the index coming to a close.

Then it happened! One of the motors sputtered. None of us was the slightest bit worried, of course. But before the motor could sputter again, we were all trying to climb out on the wing to give it artificial respiration. Then we heard a series of the most nerve-wracking sputters, but it wasn't the motor. It was Hope and myself. The motor had died.

The ship was losing altitude fast. The pilot said he was concerned.

I said, "Pleased to meet you, Concerned-- but this is hardly the time for introductions!" I was so excited that for a moment I had forgotten he was Navy Lieutenant "Fergie" Ferguson from North Hollywood, California.

Hope stood up and said with a brave laugh, "Just keep your seats, kids, there's nothing to worry about."

At this moment the other motor started to pop. Lt. Ferguson revived it, and the rest of us revived Hope.

The plane was now in a long, diving glide. I remember Hope saying that he had aged ten years in ten minutes, and that if he ever got back to the states, Paramount could use him for character parts.

Although it was a very serious situation, Bob never lost his sense of humor. He asked Ferguson how much the G.I.'s in New Caledonia paid him to dump us in the ocean.

We really shouldn't have been as upset as we were. Not even a year before, while we were touring Alaska, had we been in just as tough a spot. At that time our plane was caught in what flyers term "thick soup." As I watched the ocean coming up at us now, I asked Lt. Ferguson if he could do anything about clam chowder.

While we stood there wondering if our luck would hold out, Ferguson ordered us to throw everything nonessential overboard. Four times I had to climb back through the window. Out of the plane went all our clothes, souvenirs, books, even several cases of whisky which we were delivering to a hospital in Sydney. I had already made reservations for a room in that hospital.

Patty was very cute. In the midst of the excitement of throwing practically everything overboard, she remembered her dancing slippers. Hurriedly she opened her suitcase, removed her slippers, tied them around her neck, and threw the suitcase out of the plane. Taking a cue from Patty, Tony tied his most precious possession, his guitar, around his neck.

Not to be out-done, I twirled the ends of my mustache and tied them around my neck.

Just then Lieutenant John Sheppard, the co-pilot, came out, shouting, "We told you to get rid of everything. That miniature totem pole is no exception!"

We thought we could never convince him that he was referring to Barney Dean who stood there petrified with fear. Barney saved his own life by breaking into speech. "I've had just about enough of this trip," he moaned. "Where do I catch the Glendale bus?"

Lieutenant Ferguson shouted back from his seat, "Get ready for a crash landing."

We all sat on the floor of the plane, bracing ourselves for the impact. Lieutenant Sheppard instructed us to sit one behind the other as if we were riding a toboggan. And with that dead motor, it sounded uncomfortably like a toboggan.

We were losing altitude fast. Finally we wound up in the red. I mean the blue— we hit water.

Lieutenant Ferguson saved the insurance companies of California a lot of money. He made a great landing on a sand bar.

We were in water about knee deep. After making sure I still had my knees, I waded out. No sooner had we landed when a group of fishing boats appeared on the scene. Before anyone could open his mouth, one of the fishermen popped up with "Do you have an American cigarette?" Before he could finish the sentence he had six packs of cigarettes.

Hope said, "Where are we, and how much of an audience have we got?"

The fisherman smiled. "You have landed in Laurieton Bay on the north coast of Australia. We'll take you directly to the hotel."

"Hotel?" we all echoed in montage effect.

"You mean hot water?" shouted Hope.

"And beds?" yelled Tony.

"With sheets?" screamed Barney.

"And a tub?" cried Frances.

"With a shower?" squealed Patty.

"It's a lie!" said I.

This could not be! I had expected to be lost in an impenetrable jungle for days, maybe

HOTEL! WITH A SHOWER?
HOT WATER!!
AND A TUB!!
AND BEDS?
IT'S A LIE WITH SHEETS

weeks, maybe months, maybe years! Trekking through trackless treks on my hands, then on my knees, clutching at my burning throat. "Water!" I cried. "Water!"

Hope obliged. He pushed me off the boat into the bay.

Laurieton was a beautiful, secluded little village with grass streets where horses, pigs, chickens and cows walked around loose. It was really something out of a fairy tale book. The way we looked after our crash was really something out of a comic book.

The moment we arrived at the town Bob rushed to the nearest phone to call Sydney and tell them of our mishap. He said we wouldn't be able to get to Sydney that night but would have to stay in Laurieton. A great cheer went up. Hope stepped back from the phone, puzzled. Then he realized that the hurrahs came from the citizens of Laurieton grouped around the phone.

The Mayor insisted that we be his guests at the Victory Dance they were holding that night in the Town Hall. We gladly accepted. It was quite a celebration. Just like a New Year's Eve in Times Square, or maybe a digest version of it.

They introduced us to their new dance they called the "Hokey Pokey." Groups of eight or ten people form circles and, when the music starts, they sing the lines of the song and illustrate them with gestures.

For example, the first line of the song is "You put your right hand out." Well, you simply put your right hand out. It's as easy as that!

The next line is "You put your right hand in." Then you simply put your right hand in. No higher mathematics involved.

The following line is, and this will be quite a surprise to you, "You put your right hand out." For the corresponding gesture, see above. And while you're at it, see your dentist twice a year.

"And you turn it all about." With this line you make with your hand like you're washing a window.

You wind up the dance by placing your hands on your forehead and swinging your hips hula hula fashion. This is followed by a quick turn while you sing, "That's what it's all about."

There you have it. That's the "Hokey Pokey," and while we're at it, who's this Arthur Murray anyway?

After we Hokey-Pokeyed the night away, the Army cars came to pick us up. The men were so worn out after driving all night, that the only words they had to say to us were, "You drive back." Bob, Tony and I each got behind the wheel of a car. I had driven along for about fifty miles before one of the men woke up, turned green, and screamed, "Hey, what are you doing? Don't you know here in Australia you drive on the left side of the road?"

"Egad!" I replied, "so that's why all those trucks wound up in the ditch! And all the time I thought I was driving up the wrong side of a one-way highway!"

Apparently Hope had had the same trouble, because I looked back at his car, and there was a small truck where the radiator cap ought to be.

On and on we drove, over hill and over dale. BANG!—oh yes! and over nail.

We were so black with dust when we reached Newcastle, 280 miles away, that we didn't recognize the officer who came to meet the cars because he was so white. We soon became aware of the fact that he was Captain Lanny Ross, the famous singer.

He took one look at our dirty faces and blurted, "Haven't you heard that we don't need any more coal at Newcastle?"

All of us were exceptionally happy to see Lanny. He told us he had been assigned to our troupe as a Special Service Officer and it was his job to guide us through the last leg of our trip. Hope gave him another assignment. He was to be male lead in U. S. O. Unit #130 to sing romantic duets with Frances.

| U. S. O. UNIT | DATE | PLACE | AUDIENCE |
|---|---|---|---|
| *#130* | *August 17* | *Sydney* | *2,100* |

## THE ROAD TO AUSTRALIA or YOU SHOULD SEE SYDNEY'S GREEN STREET

WE traveled from Newcastle to Sydney in a C-47 transport plane. We had nothing against a P.B.Y., but we just didn't like the idea of checking our baggage in mid air.

Sydney went wild greeting us.

The manager of the Australia Hotel told me, "It's certainly a tribute to Bob Hope. There hasn't been this much excitement since they drove the rabbits out of New South Wales."

I said we all appreciated the Aussie enthusiasm but I wished some of them wouldn't be so over-anxious about their confetti. Twice I was hit by a telephone book somebody forgot to tear up.

When these fellows from down under give a celebration, egad! they really give it. Torn paper, flowers, hats were strewn in our path. Every once in a while the crowd would break loose and strew us.

We got along swell with the Aussies. After being around cannibals, head-hunters, and various other savages, it was a pleasure to be with people who could speak your own language.

I stopped one Australian on the street and asked him, "How goes it?"

He replied, "Oh hello, old cobber! Everything's bonzer! I'm going to shivoo tonight with a clinker that's really dinkum. Boy, what smoggin'! Well, I gotta imshi, and no chivvy."

This stopped me. I had almost forgotten how to speak English.

Suddenly it all came back to me. I retorted, "Okeh, gate, but don't be a drag, Margaret. Grab your slick chick and get your kicks, and don't inhale too much groove juice. Everything's gonna be aw reet!"

Then an aboriginal Bushman came along and translated for the two of us.

That afternoon we were invited to the home of the Governor General, Lord Wakehurst. Lady Wakehurst had done everything up just so for us: engraved invitations, just crawling with R.S.V.P.'s; receiving line, just crawling with M.P.'s (Don't get any wrong ideas. Down under, M.P. means Member of Parliament) ; also a little sedate cocktail sipping, and even chamber music. Egad! was I out of place!

We had a wonderful time, but it came to a close too soon.

We returned to our hotel. When I got to my room I found someone waiting for me. I had never seen him before. I asked him his name and he showed me a volume of the Encyclopedia Britannica.

"Don't tell me you're Clifton Fadiman," I said.

Apparently he was a famous personage, for his picture was in the Encyclopedia under the letter "K." Well, what do you know? He was a Kangaroo!

A note around the animal's neck informed me that he was a gift from a fan of mine. I grew immediately fond of the little fellow and we played hop-scotch for hours.

Without warning, the door fell in, and there stood the hotel manager. He told me

the rules of the hotel forbade me to keep a kangaroo in my room. He said the kangaroo would have to go down and register for a room of his own.

I smoothed the manager down by taking him to dinner, and eventually we became fast friends. It became one of the sights of Sydney to see the manager and myself, fast friends, racing through the streets; or strolling arm in arm down the boulevards on hot days, with my trusty kangaroo hopping along behind us, his pouch filled to the brim with nice, cool beer.

Before we boarded the plane to fly from Sydney, Hope told me I would have to leave my kangaroo behind.

I pleaded, "Oh, no—no! You can't do this to Abner!"

I called my kangaroo "Abner" because he certainly wasn't Lum, so he just had to be Abner.

Hope insisted, "That kangaroo stays here!"

"He'll be hopping mad," I warned.

Hope shook his fist at me. This moved me considerably. My neck was in his fist!

Hope said, "There is room on the plane for just one of you."

That settled it. There was no more arguing. The plane took off, circled the field, and landed again. The kangaroo had become air sick and I was permitted to take its place.

As we soared into the air, I looked back at little Abner, standing on the ground. Tears came into my eyes. He was standing with his back to me, waving goodbye with his tail.

| U. S. O. UNIT | DATE | PLACE | AUDIENCE |
|---|---|---|---|
| *#130* | *August 21* | *Hollandia* | *10,000* |

**BACK TO THE JUNGLES**
**or**
**MY LAST CHANCE TO KOHAIT**

WE left Australia via Brisbane, Townsville, and Nadsab, and arrived at Hollandia in New Guinea for the last leg of our jungle circuit. According to information received, to find the island of New Guinea you have to go to the Melanesian region of Australiasis, cross the Torres Strait and the Arafura Sea, and go around the Moluccas by the Gilolo Passage. Now that you have found New Guinea, you may have to find a new tongue.

The unknown interior of New Guinea, mostly impassable mountain chains and poisonous swamps, still waits for a man to explore it. After we had given our show, the New Guinea G.I.'s voted me the man. I welcomed the chance to kohait in the jungle once more. I was especially anxious to see the famous bird of paradise. An unidentified sergeant offered to send me to paradise by a shorter route, but I turned him down.

Putting thirty pounds of provisions into a knapsack, and putting the knapsack on my back, I fell down.

Hope removed the weight and helped me to my feet.

"Colonna," he said, "you're as weak as a two-year-old."

I protested loud and long at this libel, and made him raise the estimate by a year.

I set off into the jungle carrying only my

compass and my rifle. I always aim my rifle by compass—near-sighted!

By mid-afternoon I was at the great Mamberamo swamp. By nightfall I was at the great Mamberamo swamp. By midnight I was at the great Mamberamo swamp. Awfully sticky stuff, that swamp.

I was proud of one thing, though. I was the first white man to ever see that deadly swamp, crawling with poisonous reptiles. And I looked pretty white, too! When I thought that I had left a more or less comfortable bunk at Hollandia where I was surrounded by friends and well-wishers, to journey into this trackless jungle, I was seized by regret. A split second later I realized that it wasn't regret at all—it was a wildcat. A split lip later I was beating it home through the jungle.

When at last I crawled back to our camp, covered with mud from head to toe, I found Hope waiting up for me. He greeted me with a compliment.

"Professor," he said, "I'm glad to see that at last you're wearing clothes that accentuate your positive."

I just shrugged my shoulders, and after he had wiped the mud from his eyes, he said, "That's a dirty way to answer me."

We were joined by Lieutenant Commander George Halas, the Naval Welfare Officer assigned to our troupe in New Guinea, who was formerly coach of the Chicago Bears professional football team.

Commander Halas took us across the lake to the camp of Lieutenant General Robert L. Eichelberger and his 6th Army. On the way we passed several native huts that were built on stilts over the water. It must be quite an experience for a sleepy native to reach outside his door in the morning for the milk and come in with a jellyfish.

Before we left Hollandia we met a fantastic character. The way he acted, he met one too. He was a Dutch youth who had lived in New Guinea all his life. He was familiar with every swamp, back trail, and jungle run in the area. He had been spying on the Japs and reporting their movements for months. I tried to get in a word or two about my exploits in the jungle, but I felt Hope's hand over my mouth. So I listened politely as the boy continued his story.

He knew the lore of the jungle and could move within it without a sound. He was equally adept at disappearing into the shadow of a huge fern or swinging to the top of a tree in a flash, using trailing jungle vines.

I stared in amazement at the youth. The action had indeed been his, but the words sounded more like Edgar Rice Burroughs.

Hope and I talked to him about souvenirs, so off he went into the back country. A day later he was back with a collection of Jap guns, swords, and flags. He made a present of these to our troupe. We noticed that he had held back two identical Samurai swords. I asked him if he would consider selling them, and if so, what was his price.

"This one," he said, "is one dollar. The other is twenty dollars."

"I can't tell them apart," I said. "Why the difference in price?"

"This one I got from a *live* Jap."

To this day I get goosepimples even when I pass a Dutch Boy Paint Store.

| U. S. O. UNIT | DATE | PLACE | AUDIENCE |
|---|---|---|---|
| *#130* | *August 24* | *Wakde* | *16,000* |
| | *August 25* | *Owi* | *8,000* |
| | *August 27* | *Aitape* | *30,000* |
| | *August 28* | *Los Negros* | *22,000* |
| | *August 29* | *Endila Island* | *8,000* |
| | *August 29* | *Manus* | *8,000* |
| | *August 30* | *Ponam* | *2,500* |
| | *August 31* | *Los Negros* | *5,500* |

**ON THE EDGE OF THE BATTLE AREA**
**or**
**PARDON ME, ARE YOU USING THIS FOXHOLE?**

AFTER we bid adieu to Hollandia, we hopped around from island to island like a flea full of high octane.

First was Manus Island in the Admiralties. Originally a bare slice of coral, Manus now has huge floating dry docks as well as its own ice cream and Coca Cola plants.

While we were standing with our tongues down to our chests watching the ice cream being manufactured, Hope summed it up: "How about that! They've taken a *desert* island and turned it into a *dessert* island!"

The sight of tons and tons of chocolate, vanilla, strawberry, and pistachio brought out the pioneer in me. Wide-eyed and with mouth watering like the Colorado River in the spring, I opened the door of the giant freezer and followed my tongue inside. As I stood there ankle-deep in tutti-frutti, I gazed awe-struck at the enormous mound of vanilla ice cream looming in front of me. It was not unlike Mount Whitney with a cherry on top.

A chill of apprehension ran through me. Someone had closed the freezer door. There I was—trapped! Trapped like a rat in a hunk of cheese! Ice cream to the right of me. Ice cream to the left of me. Ice cream in front of me. And behind me—sherbert!

After much contemplation, during which I began to feel more and more like a popsicle, I finally came to a decision. There was only one route to freedom: I had to eat my way out! Of course, there was easier routes, but who's escaping? You or I? All right then. So I started eating my way out!

In the course of this escapade, I got my foot caught in the mammoth conveyer belt. It slowly dragged me toward the central mixer! I was doomed to be just another nut in the black walnut ice cream. But my life was saved by a mechanical claw which snatched me from the belt in the nick of time. It was the purpose of this machine to reject impurities. Needless to say I was the happiest impurity in the whole place.

The claw deposited me in the refuse bin outside. I was saturated with ice cream from head to toe—a veritable Colonna a la mode!

The next thing I knew Hope was shaking me back into reality.

"Colonna," he said, "are you nuts?"

"No—betel nuts!" The truth is I had been absentmindedly chewing one of those Munda Mickeys for the past ten minutes.

Once again my imagination had run away with me. The effect lingered until we arrived at the island of Sarmi where the commanding officer told us that the Japs were close by. I felt like running away without my imagination.

As we were doing the show, we could see the fighter planes and medium bombers dive-bombing a Jap stronghold only a few miles away. A few miles never seemed shorter to me in all my life.

The men in the audience kept one eye on the show and one eye on the sky. As for me, I kept one eye on the sky, one eye on the audience, one eye on my helmet, and one eye on a foxhole. Four eyes? Certainly. Once again I was beside myself!

The area around the show was a little crowded, so some of the G.I.'s climbed trees to get a better view. Right in the middle of

the show a shot rang out and whistled overhead! All the men in the trees yelled, "Sniper!", and they dropped to the ground like sacks of grain. Four of the men landed on one of the people in our troupe. Now I know how it feels to be hit by a sack of grain wearing G.I. shoes.

After Sarmi, the next stop was Aitape, where I met a number of people I knew. Much to my surprise I ran into my cousin, Sergeant Jerry Mangiacotti, and what a beautiful first name he has. He had been on guard duty at the food supply depot the night before, and during the night three Japs tried to raid the icebox for a midnight snack, so he gave it to them—right between the eyes.

Also on Aitape I met Colonel Monk Meyers, former West Point All-American and now head of an infantry outfit, and Smoky Saunders, the jockey who booted home Omaha in the 1935 Kentucky Derby.

When he enlisted in the army, Smoky signed up for the cavalry, figuring that riding was something he knew a little about. However, in a short time the army started to bring in horses by General Motors and White and International. Smoky said that at first he'd had a little trouble handling the trucks. It isn't hard to get friendly with a horse, but he didn't think it would get him anywhere to slip a lump of sugar into the carburetor. For sentimental reasons, Smoky named his truck Omaha, fitted up the driver's seat with stirrups, and played he was winning the Aitape Derby. But when he crossed the finish line, instead of a loving cup from Colonel Matt Wynn, he got another load of dirt from Sergeant Joe Smith.

*We passed greased lightning—*

From Aitape we returned to Owi, where we stayed with General Ennis C. Whitehead, Commander of the Fifth Air Force. We were made members of the Fifth Air Force Officers' Club. It's not easy to become a member of this organization. To qualify we had to take a ride in a P-61 Black Widow night fighter. The P-61 is like the P-38 only twice as. When I went up, I was locked in the back compartment of the plane. There was no inter-communication system, and I had no way of telling the pilot what to do in case of trouble. No doubt you know how fast these planes travel. They move like greased lightning. This is an understatement. We passed greased lightning like it was a spot on the rug. When we landed I told the spot to move over.

At last I was a member of the Officers' Club! I was now eligible for the privileges of the Club. I had the right to go up in a Black Widow any time I wanted. I traded that privilege for a Bromo Seltzer!

Still fizzing I joined the others, and we P.T.'d to Woendi, Endila, Lumbrum, Ponam, and finally Pitylu. Here there was a sign on the beach which read "WE PITY U ON PITYLU." Of all the islands we visited, Pitylu was the smallest. And you can cut that in half. Too big! Cut it again!

You can stand on one end of the island and see a fellow on the other end lighting a cigarette. In fact, it's your cigarette.

I was so impressed by the infinitesimal size of Pitylu that I went around searching for a man who could tell me how such a small island ever came to be. I finally found a grizzled old Marine staff sergeant who offered to enlighten me.

"Once upon a time, chum, there was in

this section of the Pacific the biggest island you ever saw. On it lived a beautiful young native princess. She had everything. The guy in love with her was strictly from hunger. He had nothing. The princess said she'd marry him on one condition: Somewhere on the island there was a magic stone. If he could find it and bring it to her, she would middle-aisle it with him.

"So this guy goes walking around the island, picking up stones, looking at them, and throwing them in the ocean. This routine goes on year after year. Gradually the island gets smaller and smaller. So what happens?

One day he finally finds the magic stone. He rushes to give it to the beautiful young princess, and call me a pumpkin if she isn't ninety-five years old!

"He gets so mad, he takes that magic stone and throws it into the ocean!—It floats, it's an island, and we're standing on it right now!"

"Amazing!" I exclaimed.

The sergeant went on to warn me, "Now, don't go passing this story around. It's strictly confidential. There's one reason why you can't tell this to a living soul."

"Why?"

"It's not true!"

You may think I have been exaggerating about the size of Pitylu. In that case you should have been with us when we were leaving. As we boarded a P.B.Y. for Los Negros, a speck flew into my eye. I was upset, but not half as much as the commanding officer who yelled at me, "Put that island back!"

At Los Negros I met two old friends of mine, Paul Mertz, who used to be an arranger for Fred Waring and Paul Whiteman, and Jimmy Fitzpatrick, a saxophonist from Boston. Jimmy and I had played in the same band in the Massachusetts metropolis and he had some wonderful news for me. He said they had forgotten my music and it was safe for me to return to Boston.

Our next stop was Madang, where we were met by a delegation of officers who asked us to do an unscheduled show at Alexishaven, some fifteen miles up the coast.

When we arrived we found that a group of American and Australian soldiers had been waiting five hours for us. They had even put out a special edition of their magazine "Fantales" in our honor.

Hope looked through a copy, and when he came across his picture, he shook his head and said, "I know the camera never lies, but it could at least be tactful!"

That night we were put on the submarine tender U.S.S. *Otus*. Before we turned in, we were invited to see a movie on the deck. By a remarkable coincidence, it was a Bob Hope picture, 'My Favorite Blonde.' This was one he did several years ago with Madeleine Carroll.

We had a hard time hearing the dialogue of the picture. Hope kept applauding and shouting, "Bravo! Bravo! Academy Award!"

In all fairness, I must admit Hope gave a terrific performance. When he stopped, we were all able to sit back and enjoy the picture.

That morning at three-thirty we were awakened and told we were going home to the States.

The States! The States! Those words had a familiar ring.

Just then I heard Hope calling from the deck, "Come on, Professor, we're leaving!"

These words also had a familiar ring.

But I couldn't leave the Pacific Islands without saying goodbye to all the wonderful friends I'd met there: the G.I.'s, the Navy men, the Marines, the Special Service Officers, the native chiefs, the head-hunters, the blister bugs, and Abner, my beloved kangaroo.

To each of these I penned the same note of farewell: "Me fella boy kohait in guvman U. S. A."

| U. S. O. UNIT | DATE | PLACE | AUDIENCE |
|---|---|---|---|
| *#130* | *September 3* | *Burbank* | *5 relatives* |

**BACK IN CALIFORNIA**
**or**
**MY SUN! MY SUN!**

WE arrived in California at the Lockheed Air Terminal, Burbank. It was late Saturday afternoon, September the 3rd.

Our families were at the airport to meet us. Hope's wife, Dolores, threw her arms around his neck while his two children, Linda and Tony, looked at me with the same frightened expressions I knew so well.

The little boy tugged at his father's sleeve and said, "Daddy, you brought him home with you? I thought you said you were going to take him over there and lose him."

We all got a laugh out of this. You know the way children are always kidding. Well, he wasn't.

My wife, Flo, kissed me tenderly on the cheek. She never was quite sure where my mouth was. Then she stepped back with my little youngster, Robert John, in her arms and allowed me to gaze my fili. My! How that child had changed! When I last saw him he was only three years old. Now he had grown to a man of three years and six weeks.

Everyone was fascinated by the souvenirs we brought back. We were really loaded down with them—Jap flags, guns, swords, bayonets, helmets.

Looking at all this military equipment, Hope remarked, "I don't see how the Japs can hold out much longer. They haven't got anything left to fight with—excepting maybe the kitchen sink."

"Ah, no!" I cried, as I pulled the kitchen sink out of my duffle bag.

Our troupe, U. S. O. Unit No. 130, had come back home. How tired, proud, and happy we were, only the other U. S. O. units will ever know.

We had played 150 shows in the Pacific Islands, flown 30,000 miles, and entertained more than a million G.I.'s.

Led by Bob Hope, our troupe's big ambition was to be with the men who needed entertainment. Wherever they were, Alaska, the Aleutians, the South Pacific, Australia, the Caribbean, Europe—that's where we wanted to be.

That was our troupe—all over!

# EPILOGUE

The following year at home was packed with activity. We split up our time doing broadcasts and visiting Army camps. The days flew by—Sunday, Monday, Pepsodent, Wednesday, Thursday, Saturday. Friday flew too fast.

It was a beautiful Spring day when Hope drew me to one side and said, "Colonna, I've got some happy news for you. Guess what?"

A sparkle came into my eyes. "We're going to Europe!"

"How did you guess?"

"I'm psychic, and besides, I saw you shove that suitcase into my hand!"

He said, "Are you happy or sad?"

I grinned. "I'm ready. Let's go!"

I was happy for the chance to find out how the other half of the G.I.'s were making out.

And so on the fifteenth of June we hit the road to Europe: Scotland, England, France, Belgium, Germany, Austria and Czechoslovakia. Though the landscape was different, we entertained the same swell bunch of guys we'd shared our mess kits with in the Pacific.

Now most of the G.I.'s I met all over the world are back home. Wherever I go in the U. S. I can expect to meet a friend from Europe or the South Pacific. And there is a question very close to my heart that only one of them can answer:

"WHO THREW THAT COCONUT?"

B·H·
PEPSODENT
TO
EUROPE
5686 1/2 Mi.
S.PACIFIC
J·C·
ALASKA
TARAWA

*. . . Still Friends?*

VINE ST
Co.
93

CPSIA information can be obtained at www.ICGtesting.com
Printed in the USA
BVOW05s1258201013

334134BV00008B/83/P